"Wait a minute," Jack said. "You dropped Susan off at her mother's and she didn't go inside?"

"I think she went inside." He looked confused. "If you mean, did I sit in the car and watch her go in, no, I didn't. I let her off—it was daylight—and while she was walking up to the door, I drove away. It's Brooklyn. It's a narrow, one-way street parked up on both sides, and there was a car behind me. I left."

It sounded perfectly reasonable. "When did you call her?" I asked.

"I don't know. Four, five o'clock. Her mother said she hadn't seen her for a couple of days."

I didn't like the cold feeling in my chest. . . .

By Lee Harris
Published by Fawcett Books:

THE GOOD FRIDAY MURDER
THE YOM KIPPUR MURDER
THE CHRISTENING DAY MURDER
THE ST. PATRICK'S DAY MURDER
THE CHRISTMAS NIGHT MURDER
THE THANKSGIVING DAY MURDER
THE PASSOVER MURDER
THE VALENTINE'S DAY MURDER
THE NEW YEAR'S EVE MURDER
THE LABOR DAY MURDER
THE FATHER'S DAY MURDER
THE MOTHER'S DAY MURDER
THE APRIL FOOLS' DAY MURDER
THE HAPPY BIRTHDAY MURDER

THE
NEW
YEAR'S
EVE
MURDER

Lee Harris

FAWCETT BOOKS • NEW YORK

A Fawcett Book
Published by The Ballantine Publishing Group
Copyright © 1997 by Lee Harris

www.ballantinebooks.com

Library of Congress Catalog Card Number: 97-90551

ISBN 0-449-15018-6

First Edition: December 1997

OPM   13   12   11   10   9   8   7   6   5

For John D. Ogden,
a great teacher

The year is going, let him go;
Ring out the false, ring in the true.

ALFRED, LORD TENNYSON
"In Memoriam"

The author wishes to thank
Ana M. Soler, James L.V. Wegman,
and Matthew G. Saltarelli, M.D.,
for their excellent information.

1

At the last minute, it was touch and go whether we would go to the party. For Jack, my husband of almost a year and a half, the evening was a tradition not to be missed, one he usually shared with old friends, both on the job with the NYPD and people he had gone to school with since he was a curly-headed child. New Year's Eve didn't have the mystique for me it had for him, the excitement that included all the trappings like champagne and noisemakers. Of course, having spent fifteen years in a convent where most of us went to sleep at nine, tired from a day that began at five, regardless of the calendar, the difference in our approach was understandable. It has only been in the two and a half years since I left St. Stephen's for a secular life that New Year's Eve has achieved a certain luster.

But the real reason for our hesitation was that we were the new parents of a baby boy who had changed our lives, separately and together, in ways we could not have imagined when an act of love had started his existence in the cold of last winter. Edward Bennett Brooks, named after my father who died when I was a child, weighing seven pounds and ten ounces (slightly less than a Sunday *Times* Jack brought home about the time of his birth) was both a Presence and a Personality almost from before his birth and certainly from the moment I heard his first cry.

What had become of my certainty that an absolutely dependable baby-sitter would enable me to teach my one-morning-a-week class at a local college? And that easygoing husband of mine who seemed unruffled in situations of life, death, and drawn weapons—where was the calm I had always counted on? How many phone calls a day from the Sixty-fifth Precinct in Brooklyn did it take to insure that his wife and son were feeling fine, eating well, taking their naps, and getting their sunshine?

I smile as I say this. Having observed friends and acquaintances from various degrees of afar as they became mothers, I blithely assumed that this next step on the path of life was a simple one, easily achievable by the smart and the not-so-smart, and even by those of us who still found putting an interesting dinner together something of a chore. It seemed easy enough. When he wakes up, you change him, feed him, change him again, talking to him, of course, to start him on his way to life in a happy family, then lay him down gently for some more sleep. But our Eddie hadn't read the same books I had. Sometimes he wasn't ready to go back to sleep after his feeding, and other times he awoke not hungry but in a mood to be entertained. I didn't mind entertaining him— it was fun and I had looked forward to it for the many months of my pregnancy. But Jack and I wondered, as evening on the last day of the year drew near, whether our hosts at the party we were planning to attend who had offered us a room with a double bed and a crib would be as accepting of our son's unpredictable schedule as we were.

In the end I called them, and they said they would be devastated if we didn't show up, so we packed our angelically sleeping baby into the car and took off.

Our hosts for the great evening were Arnold and Harriet Gold. I had met Arnold not long after I left St.

Stephen's and was investigating what turned out to be the first in a string of murders I would look into. Forty years earlier, Arnold had represented one of the presumed killers of a woman found dead in her Brooklyn apartment on Easter Sunday. My work on the case eventually turned up the real killer and led me to the precinct where I met Jack, changing my life forever. Arnold, who had been a very young lawyer at the time of the murder, was more than happy to help me out and we became good enough friends that I consider him a surrogate father. He's also my employer from time to time, which is nice because I can do most of the work at home, and I am one of those people who really need to work to keep me happy.

Jack dropped me off at the Golds' and went to find a parking space. Eddie was sleeping blissfully, and even the commotion of our entry hardly fazed him. Harriet took me upstairs to the bedroom reserved for us, and I managed to take off the baby's outer clothes and get him settled in the crib with only a few murmurs and sighs to keep me on my guard.

"He's wonderful," Harriet said in a soft voice.

"Yes, I think he is." I squeezed her.

"And he's all ours," she said with a big smile. "At least until tomorrow. Come, let's get you something to nibble."

Jack showed up a few minutes later, carrying our small suitcase and the baby seat, both of which he stowed in the bedroom, more, I thought, to check on his son than to get them out of the way. When he returned, Arnold fixed them both drinks and they sat down, probably to talk about Jack's law classes. Since I was a nursing mother, I was saving alcohol for midnight, when I planned to indulge in a gulp of champagne that I hoped would not have an adverse effect on my little one.

It was a wonderful party, thanks to the interesting and diverse guests who kept coming as the New Year neared. I spent some time talking to a lawyer whose name I had seen often enough in the *Times* to know he was famous and very special, a man who said of Arnold all the things I had come to know, that he was a truly admirable human being who would take any case he believed in and who never gave up until he was convinced that the truth had been made known.

"You'd be surprised how many hopeless cases Arnold has won," the lawyer said with feeling.

"A lot more than I know about," I said. "He's remarkably modest when it comes to talking about himself."

"He also knows the best lawyer jokes," he said with a twinkle. "I think he generates them in that little office of his. How do you come to know him?"

I explained our relationship.

"Ah, the case of the twins with mental retardation. Took him forty years to set that one straight. So you're the one who did the digging."

"It was quite an experience."

We talked for some time, and he told me about some of his more interesting cases. I wondered if Jack would ever be in that position, talking to someone at a party about his cases—a very sweet thought.

I don't know when I became aware that there was an undercurrent of something amiss, but I remember sensing it. The phone rang several times during the evening, and Harriet answered it, but at least once she came into the living room to speak to Arnold, and he left the room quickly, looking troubled.

A little after ten, the Golds' daughter looked around the room and asked, "Does a crying baby belong to anyone here?" and I jumped up and dashed for the stairs. Eddie was waiting to be fed, and I sat in a lovely old rocking chair and nursed him till he fell asleep, which I almost did, too. As I was putting him back in the crib, I heard Arnold's voice on the other side of the interior bedroom wall.

"I'm here, Ada," his muffled voice said, and then there were silences and more muffled questions and comments.

I felt the chill of bad news, of a woman's anxiety, of the need to call a lawyer friend on this most celebrated night of the year. Had someone been hurt? Arrested? I didn't want to know. I patted my sleeping baby and waited till the conversation was over before going downstairs. I didn't want to meet Arnold as he left his room, full of whatever he had been told on the telephone. When I reached the living room, he was talking to Harriet. A moment later he was circulating among his guests.

Someone turned on the television set just before midnight so we would have the time right. There was Times Square, a place I had walked through during the day on a few occasions and once or twice at night with Jack. Tonight it was packed with more people than lived in my town and all the towns around it, many of them holding up banners with distant cities and states printed in large letters that the camera panned across. Here was Ohio, there was Kansas. I have seen very little of my country outside the New York City area, and just thinking of people traveling such a long way to watch a lighted ball drop as the New Year began excited me. Kansas, the center of the United States. Cornfields and polite people and plenty of parking spaces. I smiled.

"We're gettin' there," Jack said, suddenly at my side just when I needed him.

"Can you imagine coming all the way from Kansas to celebrate the New Year?"

"To the Big Apple? Sure. Except they must be

freezing their fingers and toes off tonight. It's cold out there."

"Maybe we'll go there someday."

"Times Square?"

"Kansas."

Jack laughed. "Wait till Eddie's out of diapers."

"I bet that would be fun."

"Sixty seconds, honey."

I watched the countdown, my glass half-full of bubbling champagne, the ball slowly descending. My heart was in my mouth. I was starting my first full year as a mother. I was in the company of the most fascinating people I had ever met. I was happier at this moment than I had ever been.

"Happy New Year!" The greeting rang out in chorus. Jack and I kissed, then kissed again. I hung onto my glass, lest I lose the little I had allotted for myself on this special evening. Then we drank and joined in a happy chorus of *Auld Lang Syne*. I found myself kissing an assortment of men and women, the famous lawyer, a rather infamous lawyer, a doctor I had chatted with earlier whose wife was a lawyer, and finally Arnold himself, a great hug and a heartfelt kiss.

"You teary-eyed or bleary-eyed?" he asked.

"A little of both. It's been such a great year, and the new one's going to be a wonderful one."

"Well enjoy it, Chrissie. You deserve the best."

"You, too, Arnold."

To my surprise there was a midnight buffet. After hours of indulging in delicious tidbits, one of my favorite ways of eating, I saw Harriet put out a great spread of hot and cold dishes and invite us all to help ourselves.

"It looks wonderful, Harriet," I said, helping her carry a few small things out to the dining room table. "When did you have time to do all this?"

"I didn't," she said proudly. "I had it catered. And you know who I used? Jack's sister."

"You're kidding."

"Arnold said, why not keep it in the family. She did such a great job at your wedding, I've been looking for an excuse to hire her. I made her promise she wouldn't say a word. Isn't it beautiful?"

"Fabulous."

"Go and eat. It's all nourishing, I promise. And if you feel too tired to stay awake, you can disappear any time you want."

By now I had my second wind. Without thinking of how I would feel in the morning, I ate heartily, talked ambitiously, and had a plain old good time. When at last I saw my usually energetic husband stifle a yawn, I looked at my watch and knew the time had come. The crowd had thinned out, and now I didn't have to excuse myself repeatedly as I edged toward him.

"Chris," he said with some surprise as I reached him.

"Forgot that I was here?"

"Just a lot of good conversation. This is Abel Gardner, a friend of Harriet's."

We said our hellos.

"Must be getting late," Jack said. "I'm starting to feel done in."

I picked up my cue and we retired to our upstairs quarters.

I was hoping Eddie would choose this night to sleep through his two A.M. feeding for the first time. He was more than a month old, but less than six weeks, and my pediatrician had warned me not to count on sleeping through the night too soon. And he was right. Just as I was about to get into bed, Eddie was up with a bang, so I didn't get to sleep till close to three. And then, just as I fell into a deep, necessary sleep, I heard the phone ring in the next room. It was answered with a soft voice and I turned over and went back to sleep, but I knew I had been right and that somewhere, something was very wrong.

The three Brookses were up early, only one of us with any enthusiasm for starting a new day. I kept Eddie as quiet as I could while Jack and I dressed. Then we all went downstairs to let the family sleep. It was a bright, sunny day with almost no snow to be seen out the front windows. Back in Oakwood we had shoveled a path to the door and to the garage, but here, what had fallen a few days earlier had largely melted.

"Up already?" It was Harriet Gold, dressed in a wool skirt and a tailored shirt and looking as energetic as my son. "Come here, you sweetheart." She picked him up out of his little seat and hugged him and talked to him while he watched in wide-eyed interest. "What a doll you are," she said finally, putting him back in his chair. "Breakfast, folks?"

We joined her in the kitchen as she made coffee and set the table.

"My daughter probably won't be down till this afternoon, so let's find some good stuff here and enjoy ourselves."

"Is Arnold still sleeping?" I asked.

"Arnold's gone. I don't know when he'll be back."

"I hope he's not working."

She looked a little odd. "I hope it doesn't turn out to be work. There's a problem, and he's gone to see if there's anything he can do."

"The phone calls," I said.

"I hope they didn't wake you. Our friend is rather distraught."

I was about to answer when the doorbell rang.

"I don't believe this," Harriet said. "It's New Year's Day. What's wrong with people?" She wiped her hands on a towel and went to the door. "Well, you've missed him," I heard her say. "Come on in anyway and join us for breakfast."

She came into the kitchen with a dark-haired, rather good-looking man in his thirties. "This is Kevin Angstrom," she announced. "Chris and Jack Brooks. And little Eddie Brooks, who's joining us this morning."

Kevin Angstrom seemed less than impressed with our son. He looked worried, and I sensed he didn't want to be here if Arnold wasn't. He said a perfunctory hello, then leaned against the doorjamb. "Do you know when he'll be back?" he asked.

"He's gone to see Susan's mother."

A sibilant of an obscenity whistled through his teeth. "She told me to come here to talk to him."

"Well, he'll be back, Kevin. Just sit down and maybe we can make some sense of this." Harriet took some great-smelling muffins out of the toaster oven. Jack had taken over the eggs, and he turned the flame off just as everything else was ready for the table.

"Kevin's significant other wasn't where she was supposed to be yesterday," Harriet said by way of explanation. "She's the daughter of a friend of ours."

"She's missing?" Jack asked, never one to allow a polite circumlocution to obscure an unpleasant truth.

"Since yesterday afternoon or maybe the day before," Kevin said. "Just coffee, please." He sat in the spot that Arnold would have taken.

"I'm a detective sergeant with NYPD," Jack said. "When did you last see her?"

Kevin's face brightened when he heard Jack's identity. "The day before yesterday. I dropped her off at her mother's. She was going to stay overnight, and I would pick her up for a party we were going to last night."

"Kevin called Susan at her mother's yesterday, and Susan wasn't there," Harriet said.

"And she hadn't spent the night there."

"Wait a minute," Jack said. "You dropped her off at her mother's and she didn't go inside?"

"I think she went inside." He looked confused. "If you mean, did I sit in the car and watch her go in, no, I didn't. I let her off—it was daylight—and while she was walking up to the door, I drove away. It's Brooklyn. It's a narrow, one-way street parked up on both sides, and there was a car behind me. I left."

It sounded perfectly reasonable. "When did you call her?" I asked.

"I don't know. Four, five o'clock. Her mother said she hadn't seen her for a couple of days."

I didn't like the cold feeling in my chest. "What's the neighborhood like?"

"It's as safe at this one," Harriet said. "Private houses, children playing in the street, mothers pushing strollers."

"But you never know," Kevin said.

"Does she have a car?" Jack asked.

"No, but she drives."

"Her mother have a car?"

"Yes. I'm sure if it were missing, she would have said."

"Ada called us several times last night," Harriet said. "She didn't say anything about the car being missing."

"Let me just get this straight," I said. As I spoke, I glanced over at the baby seat where Eddie was resting, his eyes glued to my face as I spoke. I smiled in spite of myself. "Two days ago, in the afternoon or evening—"

"Late afternoon," Kevin interjected.

"—you dropped Susan off at her mother's house. You think she went inside but you can't swear to it."

"Right."

"Yesterday about four, you called her there, to make plans for New Year's Eve."

"And she wasn't there and her mother hadn't seen her for a couple of days."

"Could she have slept over without her mother knowing she was there?"

He thought about it. "Sure. She's a grown-up. If her mother came home late and Susan was already asleep, maybe she wouldn't have noticed."

"Is there a father there?" I asked.

"There is definitely a father," Harriet said. "A good and caring father."

"We'll have to talk to them, Harriet. A young woman missing in the city scares me."

"Me, too," she said quietly, looking away.

"Scares the hell out of me." Kevin walked out of the kitchen, as though he had had enough.

"It's very unlike Susan," Harriet said. "I don't want to be an alarmist, but I'm worried."

Jack started to say something when we all heard the key turn in the lock, and then Arnold's voice saying, "I'm home."

"Come on in, honey," Harriet called, leaving the kitchen.

"I've got Ada with me. Jack and Chris still here?"

I knew what was coming next.

2

Ada Stark was a tall, good-looking woman in her late fifties or early sixties. Her thick, short hair was salt-and-pepper with a lot more pepper than salt, and she had a clear complexion that today was devoid of makeup except for lipstick.

We had all been introduced and were arranged around the living room, where last night the New Year had been ushered in loudly and happily.

"Two nights ago," Ada said. She pressed her fingertips to her forehead as if to conjure up the memory of the second-last night of the year. "I met Ernie for dinner in Manhattan. I've been over this with Arnold already, you know."

"Humor us," Arnold said. "I want Jack and Chris to hear what happened."

"We weren't back that late, nine maybe, nine-thirty. I turned the news on at ten so I'm sure we were back by then."

Eddie suddenly started to cry.

"He's tired," I said.

"I'll take him," Harriet offered. She picked him up, talking to him like a doting grandmother. He stopped crying and laid his head on her shoulder, as I watched with a mixture of hope that he would let her care for him and an unexpected flash of resentment that someone was successfully taking over my sacred task.

"Go on," Arnold said. "You know you were home before ten. Did you have any idea Susan was coming home to sleep?"

"None. She has a key, she has a room, she keeps clothes in it, changes the bedding when she wants to. Sometimes she calls to say she's coming, sometimes she just pops in. I had no idea she was coming this time. She hadn't called."

"Any deliveries during the day?" Jack asked.

She shook her head. "No meter readers either."

"Wouldn't you have seen her bedroom door closed if she were there?" I asked.

"I wouldn't. It's an old house and the floor plan is crazy. To get to her room you have to go around a corner. I had no reason to look for her, so I didn't."

"So we have no way of knowing whether she spent the night in your house or just dropped in and left before you got home."

"We don't even know if she ever set foot in the house," Ada said. "Kevin didn't see her go in. Or maybe she went in and then out again."

"How did you come to drive her?" I asked Kevin.

"I left work a little early. It was our last work day of the year. We were closed all day yesterday. Susan told me in the morning she wanted to go to Brooklyn, so I drove her. I just didn't want her taking the subway."

"What kind of mood was she in?"

"Great. She's a very 'up' person."

"What did you talk about?"

"The party we were going to. Whether the couple giving it would ever get married." He thought a moment. "Some personal things. I don't think they'd matter to you." He turned to Jack. "What's going to happen if I report her disappearance to the police?"

"Not a whole lot unless there's evidence of foul play. When a child disappears, we raise heaven and earth to find it. With an adult, it's different. Adults have the right to go where they please and not ask permission or leave word."

I had heard it all before and knew it was true. Even though you know in your heart your friend/lover/ brother/sister would never go anywhere without telling you, the police see it differently. You can't invade an adult's privacy by seeking him out when he doesn't want to be found, and you certainly can't force him to return to a place he doesn't want to be, even if he's been there his whole life.

"She didn't have a suitcase with her when I left her at her mother's, so she couldn't have been planning to go to a hotel. She wouldn't just go somewhere without packing a bag."

"Kevin's right," Ada said. "Susan's very particular. She wants to put on clean clothes in the morning; she hates sleeping on the floor if a friend is short on beds."

"Could she have packed a bag at your house?" I asked.

Ada thought. "She has clothes there, that's true, but I honestly don't know if she kept a bag in her closet. We're an independent bunch and we don't interfere with each other. I don't go through her closets any more than she goes through mine."

"So we don't know if she's missing one day or two," Jack said.

No one answered. Then Kevin said, "We're getting nowhere. How are we going to find out what happened to her?"

"I've called everyone I could think of," Ada said. "I couldn't reach them all because last night was New

Year's, but the ones I talked to hadn't seen her. Susan knows lots of people I've never met, but maybe Kevin knows some of them."

"This is getting us nowhere," he said again. "She didn't go off and visit a friend. Something happened to her. If she was visiting a friend, she would have called. She's somewhere where she can't call. Doesn't anybody see that there's a problem here?" He turned to Jack. "And you tell me the cops won't look for her because her privacy is more important than her safety. What kind of sense does that make?"

Jack started to answer, but I interrupted him. "Kevin, could we talk in another room?"

He looked around as though he wanted someone to tell him what to do. Then he said, "Sure," and he followed me to the kitchen, where I shut the door. We sat at the table.

"What is your relationship with Susan?" I started out.

"If you mean are we sleeping together, yes, we are."

"That's only a small part of what I meant. Are you living together?"

"More or less."

"Does Susan have an apartment of her own?"

"Not anymore. She stays with her folks sometimes for a few days."

"So if I asked Susan for her phone number, she'd give me the one in your apartment."

"Right."

"And how long has that been true?"

"Almost a year. She gave up her apartment at the end of January of last year."

"And she's always gone home from time to time and stayed overnight?"

"Always. She's close to her family."

"When I asked you if you were living together, why did you say 'more or less'?"

"Because . . . " The question had troubled him. "Because there was nothing formal between us. We played the your-place-or-mine game for a while and then when her lease came up for renewal, she said it was silly to pay for two apartments when she could stay with me or go home to Brooklyn. So she moved her stuff into my place."

I could see why it griped him. It hadn't been a matter of "I can't live apart from you any longer." It had been a matter of convenience, of economy, or so he had made it sound.

"Are you in love with her, Kevin?"

"Yes," he said angrily.

"And Susan?"

"We are in love with each other, OK?"

"Kevin, you said before that on the way to Brooklyn you talked about some personal things that had nothing to do with any of us."

"That's right."

"Do you think those things could have anything to do with her disappearance?"

"I don't see how." He got up from the table, took a glass out of the cabinet, and filled it with tap water. He stood near the sink drinking it while I wondered whether he was trying to delay my next questions or find an acceptable answer to my last one. Finally he put the glass in the sink. "Anything else?"

"Were you having an argument?" I asked.

"No, goddammit," he exploded. "We weren't having an argument, we weren't fighting, we were on very good terms, and we were having a conversation. And who the hell are you to be asking me all these questions?"

"I'm an amateur," I admitted, "but I've done some

investigating, some successful investigating. And I thought you might be more comfortable talking to me than to a crowd."

"I just want to find her," he said. "I have a terrible feeling someone came along after I drove away and got her attention and grabbed her. I don't think she ever got inside her mother's house."

"Why do you think that?"

"That car that was behind me," he said. "The reason that I drove off before Susan got to the door. There was a car behind me and there wasn't room for him to pass. When I got to the corner and stopped at the stop sign, there wasn't any car behind me."

"You looked for it?"

"I looked in the mirror. I remember thinking that the guy must have found a place to park on the street or else he turned into a driveway. And then I forgot about it. It was just one of those things that passes through your mind and then it's gone." There was a sound in his voice of great sadness, perhaps, I thought, of great loss.

Harriet had returned to the living room. Eddie was asleep upstairs, she told me, and she had just taken a little time to sit and watch him, to enjoy seeing him sleep. Jack had a quick conversation with Kevin and said he would accompany him to the precinct to report Susan's disappearance, with the hope that if Jack went along, it would give some impetus to the investigation.

They put their coats on and left, leaving the Golds, Ada Stark, and me in the living room. Ada looked worse than before I had gone to the kitchen. It was as if the enormity of her daughter's disappearance had begun to sink in.

"Ada," I said, "where is your husband?"

"Ernie's at the office. When he can't cope, he goes to work."

"You said you met him for dinner in Manhattan two days ago. Did you drive in?"

"I was already there. I work in the city."

"Had your husband driven in?"

"Yes. He likes to take the car. He has a lot he's been parking in for years, and the men there buff the car up and keep it looking nice for him."

"So even if Susan wanted to borrow your car, it wasn't there for her."

"That's right. It was in Manhattan." Her brow furrowed.

"Does Susan have a key to the car?"

"She's always had one."

"Is that your only car?"

"Yes."

"Do you drive?"

"Of course." She said it as though I were foolish to think otherwise.

"So it looks as though whatever happened to Susan, she didn't take the car," Arnold said.

"What about yesterday?" I asked. "Could she have slept in your house, gotten up early and driven off?"

"I used the car yesterday."

"And it was there when you looked for it?"

"It was there."

"Sounds like we've pretty much covered the obvious," Arnold said. "Let's wait and see what they accomplish at the police station."

We sat back and relaxed a little. Harriet said she would serve lunch whenever anyone was hungry, and lunch would be last night's leftovers, not a bad spur-of-the-moment meal. No one was ready to eat, so Arnold turned on his favorite music station and sat back with his eyes closed.

"He's a very nice young man," Ada said. "Kevin. He's the nicest person Susan's ever gone out with."

"She'll turn up," Arnold said. "I love Vivaldi. I could listen to him all day."

"Close your eyes, Arnold," Harriet said. "You didn't sleep much, and you were out of the house at the crack of dawn."

"I should be leaving." Ada stood.

"Wait till Jack gets back," I said. "We'll drive you." I offered mostly because I didn't want Arnold to leave his chair. But I thought it wouldn't be a bad idea to see where the Starks lived.

"It'll be out of your way."

"It won't. Sit and enjoy the music."

"I'm too worried to enjoy anything." She sat and pressed her lips together.

"Was anything worrying Susan?" Harriet asked, a question I wanted to ask myself, but it was better coming from an old friend.

"What could worry a young, successful girl who has her whole life ahead of her?"

"Maybe her relationship with Kevin," I suggested.

"I really don't think so. I think they have a beautiful relationship."

"What about your husband? Does he agree?"

"He likes Kevin very much."

I let it lie. Enough was enough. Arnold was right: We had done the obvious to death. The things I wanted to know about Susan I wasn't going to find out from her mother and her boyfriend. Maybe if Kevin got desperate enough he would tell me what they had been talking about in the car, or maybe it was true that it had nothing to do with Susan's disappearance. But Ada didn't know about that conversation, and if her face reflected her feelings, she was sick with worry.

Eventually I fed Eddie, and Harriet fed the rest of us. It took Jack and Kevin longer than I had expected, but even though traffic was light on the holiday, bureaucracies remain bureaucracies and the precinct was probably understaffed. When they finally returned, Ada was pacing and Arnold was snoring lightly in his chair.

Jack had a healthy snack, and even Kevin grabbed a bite as I got together baby and belongings. We said rather long good-byes, Arnold awakening in time to see us go.

"Let the police handle this," he warned me. "You have enough to do."

"I have a telephone, Arnold. Maybe I can make some calls from home."

"We'll talk."

As we went out to the car, Jack said quietly in my ear, "When we get there, go inside with her and get a picture of Susan. Kevin took one out of his wallet at the station house."

"OK."

"And find out where she works."

"Fine."

"She's twenty-eight and she's a good-looking gal. I don't like this at all."

I didn't either, but I wasn't sure how much I could do to help.

The Starks' house was on a quiet, one-way street, just as Kevin had described it. The houses on the street were old and different from each other, constructed in a time before builders put up identical structures by the dozen. I went inside with Ada and she found a picture for me, slipping it out of its frame.

"She's beautiful," I said.

Ada nodded, her eyes filling.

I looked at her face. "She looks just like you. People must notice the resemblance all the time."

"They do," she said, her voice hoarse. "Come upstairs with me."

I followed her up gleaming hardwood stairs and saw immediately what she meant about Susan's room. It was truly around a corner.

"In the summer I come in here and open a window to get cross-ventilation. But in the winter I don't come in so much. The cleaning woman goes in to dust, but yesterday wasn't her day. Chris, something's happened to Susan. She was never here. Look around. Does this room look as though someone used it?"

I had to admit it didn't. It was neat, the bed made, no shoes on the floor, no pencils on the schoolgirl's desk. It looked like a guest room waiting for a guest.

I walked to the closet. "May I?"

"Go ahead."

There were spring and summer clothes hanging on the rod. Susan used this closet to store her out-of-season clothes. On the floor was a pair of worn sneakers. I picked them up.

"She left those here for something to change into," Ada said. "And there are jeans in the drawer." She went and opened a dresser drawer.

There were jeans, shirts, and sweaters, all looking rather worn but comfortable. In another drawer were socks and underclothes. I walked over to the desk and opened drawers. They were filled not with the usual stationery items, but with mementoes of Susan's childhood: a blue ribbon from a camp contest, a high school award for an essay, stacks of old report cards from grade school.

"Those things go back to kindergarten," her mother said.

"Does she look at them often?"

"I doubt it. She just wanted a safe place to keep them.

She has a strong sense of who she is and where she comes from."

"That's very nice."

"It is, yes. Are you looking for anything special?"

"I'm never sure what I'm looking for," I admitted. "When I see something important, it usually leaps out at me. I don't think I'll find anything here if these are all old keepsakes."

Ada opened the top center drawer. "She keeps some pens and pencils here and there should be a pad somewhere." She closed the drawer and opened one on the left side that I hadn't looked in. "This is it." She pulled out a pad of white paper with "Notes from Susan Stark" printed in black across the top. "She uses this for informal notes. She has a lot more in Kevin's apartment."

It didn't tell me much. I looked quickly through the remainder of the drawers, but I was starting to worry about Jack alone in the car with Eddie. What I was worried about, I couldn't say. Jack had become a wonderful father overnight, so full of patience that I was astounded.

"May I take a page from the pad?" I asked.

"Of course."

I ripped off the top page and held it with the photograph. Then I took a quick look around the room. On the night table was an electric clock. I picked it up. The alarm was set for seven. "Did Susan get up at seven when she went to work?"

"About that time."

"I don't suppose you heard the alarm yesterday morning?"

Ada shook her head. "I know it sounds strange, but this is a very solidly built house and I've never heard Susan's alarm, not when she was a schoolgirl and not in recent years."

"When did you get up yesterday?"

"Maybe eight. Ernie wanted to go in for a short day, and I made breakfast for us."

"Any dishes in the sink?" I asked with faint hope.

She shook her head. "I wish I could say something that would be helpful."

"Don't worry about it. I'll be in touch, Ada."

"Thank you." She started out of the room and I followed her.

"Will you give me the names and phone numbers of Susan's friends? And where she works?"

"I'll give you what I have. Kevin can probably give you much more. He's more up to date on who Susan knows."

I was pretty sure Jack had asked Kevin but I said, "I'll give him a call."

Downstairs, I waited while Ada wrote. I walked to the windows in the living room and looked out on the street. I could see Jack in our double-parked car. He was sitting at the wheel without moving, which meant that Eddie wasn't crying. A car came from the left and I watched as it swerved to pass Jack's car. It wasn't as tight a squeeze as all that.

"Here's the best I can do." Ada gave me a sheet of paper. "Her best friend since public school, her phone number at work, and the name of the person she works with most closely. She's with a new magazine called *Single Up*. This last name is a teacher she had in fifth grade whom she's stayed close to, Mrs. Halliday. I guess they just clicked when Susan was ten. She may be retired now, I'm not sure. Susan has lots of other friends, but their names wouldn't be in my address book."

"I understand. Thank you, Ada. We'll do the best we can."

She nodded and smiled tightly. On impulse, I hugged her. Then I went outside to the car where half my family slept and the other half kept watch.

3

"Kevin said something was bothering Susan."

We were driving home and Jack had begun to tell me what he had learned this morning.

"Is that what they were talking about in the car when he drove her to the Starks'?"

"It may be. He wasn't all that forthcoming."

"I'm glad you got a chance to talk to him alone. He was resentful that I was asking him questions. I don't blame him. I just thought he might open up one-on-one away from the crowd."

"He did with me on the way to the station house. But there's a lot he didn't say."

"Like what was bothering Susan?"

"Right. It's possible he doesn't know, Chris, and it's possible he's ticked that she didn't tell him. You get anything from Ada?"

"A picture and three phone numbers, one of a fifth-grade teacher."

"You gotta be kidding."

"Ada says they clicked when Susan was ten and they stayed close. If nothing else pans out, I'll give her a call. I want to try Susan's best friend and her coworker."

"Sounds like a good place to start. I'm not sure NYPD's going to be much of a help. The detective who took the complaint was half asleep. I looked around the squad room and dorm and found a guy I'd known in the Six Five a couple of years back and asked him to help, but who knows?"

"I was looking out the Starks' front window while Ada was writing down those names. Did you see how easily that car passed you?"

"I did and it bothered me. Kevin said he dropped Susan off and kept driving because someone was behind him and couldn't get by."

"And when he got to the stop sign at the corner, the car wasn't behind him. Maybe it was one of those four-wheel-drive monsters that came up behind him. Maybe he thought the guy couldn't pass, and he was a courteous driver and kept going."

"Maybe he isn't telling the truth."

I was quiet for a moment. If Jack wasn't born suspicious, his work has certainly trained him to be. It pains me to think that a young woman's lover could do something terrible to her. Whether it pains Jack or not, he thinks about these things. "Maybe," I said grudgingly.

"It still doesn't tell us where she is. And even if he did something that we don't want to think about, he announced her disappearance to the world yesterday afternoon when he called the Starks and asked for her."

"Which gave him twenty-four hours."

"More than enough to do a lot of those things we don't want to think about."

"Let's not think about those things we don't want to think about. If he's—done something to her, it's too late to help. Let's try to figure out where she might have gone if something was bothering her."

"Home's a good place to start."

"And she didn't go there." I described the bedroom I had looked at, with its peculiar place in the house, its almost soundproof location. "At least, not that her mother heard or saw."

"No one's talked to the father yet."

"I know. But if he heard anything, wouldn't he have said something to his wife when he knew his daughter was missing?"

"Sounds reasonable."

"The room looked as though no one had been there, Jack. There wasn't a thing out of line, no dirty socks on the floor, no open book on the night table."

"They said Susan was very particular, remember? Maybe she gathered up her dirty clothes and took them with her."

Eddie sighed in his sleep and I twisted around to look at him. He looked at peace with the world. I turned back. "I'm going to make some phone calls, Jack. I don't know how far I can push this, and maybe Susan will turn up by herself and save everyone a lot of agony, but I'm worried."

"That makes two of us."

"I'll start when we get home. I can call the best friend and see what she has to say."

We drove for a while without talking. It was New Year's Day, and there were football games that had no interest for me but held my husband in thrall. He turned one on and I let the drone send me off. I was very fearful about what had happened to Susan Stark. There were a lot of questions I hadn't asked about her, but from what I had heard, she sounded like a sober human being, employed at an interesting job, living with an attractive man, on good terms with her parents. If she drank too much or used drugs, they hadn't kept her from living what appeared to be a normal, productive life. The last time I had looked for a missing woman, she had turned up dead, and I didn't want the same outcome for Susan

Stark. Almost more than that, I didn't want to be the one who found her.

"I know what you're thinking," Jack said.

"I'm not hiding it very well, am I?"

"Chris, her disappearance doesn't necessarily mean she's dead."

"But it's not a good sign."

"You'd be surprised how many young women get cold feet before making a commitment to a man, and their solution is to get away for a while and sit and think by themselves. Of course," he added in a lighter vein, "you never had qualms about me because I was such a catch."

I smiled in spite of myself. "It was that curly hair."

"And the great smile. I worked a spell over you."

I patted his thigh through his coat. "Kevin seems like such a nice guy."

"We all do, honey. When we're courting a gal, we're all angels."

I wanted to disagree with him, point out that Susan was living with Kevin and therefore knew him well, but it was an empty argument. I would get busy when we got home.

Eddie had had whatever sleep he needed for the day, and he was fairly content to be in his little seat and look around. I had no cooking to do today because Harriet had wrapped up enough goodies to keep us fed for a couple of days, so I talked to my little son for a while and then Jack took him upstairs. Jack's law school semester was over, but he liked to keep ahead in his reading in case time was at a premium next term. There were days when he was called out on a case and couldn't get away in time for his evening classes, causing him to miss one altogether or walk in late, not a pleasant experience. I heard him telling Eddie that now they would go upstairs and Daddy would hit the books. I decided to hit the telephone.

I dialed the number for Rachel Stone, Susan's best friend, and, it appeared, her oldest. It rang several times before she picked up.

"Hello?" It was a drowsy voice and I had pangs of guilt. People who stayed up very late on New Year's Eve slept very late on New Year's Day. But this late?

"Is this Rachel Stone?"

"Uh-huh."

"My name is Chris Bennett. I'm a friend of Susan Stark's mother."

"Is something wrong?"

"Susan hasn't been seen for a couple of days and her parents are worried."

"That's impossible." The voice was now fully awake. "I just talked to her."

"When was that?"

"Uh, day before yesterday."

"That's the last time she was seen."

"Have you talked to Kevin?"

"Kevin's the last person who saw Susan."

"I don't believe this. They were going to a party on New Year's Eve. She was staying in Brooklyn with her folks the night before. She told me on Wednesday when she called me."

"She told you she was staying in Brooklyn Wednesday night?"

"Yes. She even said—hold on a minute. Would you give me your name and phone number? I want to call Mrs. Stark and make sure this is on the up-and-up."

I spelled it out for her and we hung up. It was more

than fifteen minutes before she called back, and I assumed she must have had a conversation with Ada Stark.

"She said it's OK," Rachel said. "You'll have to excuse me. I didn't get that much sleep, and I really didn't know who I was talking to."

"That's OK. I'm glad you checked. Do you have some time to talk now?"

"Yes. I just made myself some coffee so I'll be human in a couple of minutes. Mrs. Stark said Susan never came home on Wednesday."

"That's the way it looks. Her mother didn't see or hear her, and the bedroom looks as if no one's been there recently."

"That's the way her room always looks. In an age of disorder, Susan's an anomaly."

"If she went somewhere by herself, can you think of where she would go?"

"I can't imagine Susan going anywhere by herself. If I decided to see a movie, I'd go to the theater and buy a ticket. If she wanted to see one, she'd call someone up for company. Susan doesn't do things alone."

"Maybe she was meeting someone at her mother's house."

There was a moment of silence. "I don't know who," Rachel said. "Not many people live in the old neighborhood anymore. You know, they grew up and went away, moved on. Even the parents of a lot of our old friends are gone now. I don't mean they've died, they've just left Brooklyn."

"What about her old fifth-grade teacher?"

"Mrs. Halliday? I think she still lives in Brooklyn but not where the Starks live."

"Rachel, tell me how you got to know Susan."

"That goes way back. It was one of the first days of

kindergarten, if you can believe it, and the teacher arranged us alphabetically, so Stone was next to Stark. We'd never laid eyes on each other before and we just became friends that day. We lived in each other's houses—well, my family lived in an apartment—and it's never flagged. We went to different colleges but we spent our vacations together. We're friends, what can I tell you?"

"It sounds as though you know each other very well."

"Better than anyone else does. I know Susan better than Kevin, better than her mother, but mothers never really know us, do they?"

It wasn't a question I could answer easily. My own mother had died when I was fourteen. "How was she getting on with Kevin?"

"She loved him. He's a great person. He's perfect for her. They complement each other in a lot of ways and they're similar in a lot of other ways. Susan's a little on the quiet side—you can probably tell I'm not—and he lets her be herself. But he also draws her out."

"You said Susan was a person who wouldn't see a movie by herself, that she'd look for company. The person you've just described sounds like someone who'd like to be alone."

"Maybe I didn't make myself clear. She likes to know someone's there but she doesn't want to talk all the time. She just likes to feel that she's not alone."

I could empathize with Susan. Even when Jack is upstairs with his books, where I can't see him or hear him, there's a kind of comfort in knowing he's there. "Is she fearful of anything?" I asked.

"Not that she ever told me."

"Do you think there was a problem with Kevin that could have popped up recently or just come to a head?"

She was silent again. "I didn't see anything," she said carefully, "and she didn't tell me anything."

"Did you sense it? Did you feel it? Rachel, your friend has been missing for forty-eight hours and no one has the slightest idea what's become of her."

"She was concerned about something," Rachel said, "but it wasn't Kevin."

"Did she tell you what it was?"

"No. I sensed it."

"Could you sense what it was?"

"It wasn't work, it wasn't Kevin. I think it was Susan's own personal demon."

It was an exasperating comment. "You're not making this easy for me," I said more lightly than I felt.

"I don't really know how to say this, and what I'm going to tell you may have nothing to do with Susan's disappearance, but she had a childhood fear that grew to be a grown-up fear, maybe more of a concern. When Susan was a little kid, she got it into her head that she was adopted."

"She's the image of her mother," I said, arguing with someone who I was sure didn't believe it any more than I did. "I have a picture of her."

"Well, sure, and she knows that. You don't have to be a geneticist to figure out that she's Ada Stark's daughter. But we're not talking facts here, we're talking about a kid's fear."

"Rachel, do you remember when she first told you about this fear? Do you remember anything that happened around that time that could have scared her?"

"It was so long ago. We were just kids."

"Could her mother have gotten angry with her and said something she shouldn't have?" I didn't really believe this was a possibility but I had to ask.

"Mrs. Stark? She's the most sensible woman I've ever met. I don't think so."

"Well, what about Susan's father?"

"He's pretty cool too. I don't think so."

"Do you know him well?"

"I told you, I lived at their house when Susan wasn't living at mine. I saw them in pajamas, I saw them mad, I saw them every way you can imagine."

"I just asked because Mr. Stark seems to have secreted himself in his office. His wife said he does that when he's worried."

"Yeah," Rachel agreed. "Probably true. He's kind of a quiet person—Susan may look like her mother but she's her father's girl. When he has something to say, he'll come out of his cocoon."

"Let's get back to Susan's fear," I said. Something in the back of my brain had begun nagging at me. What if my new baby someday decided I had not given birth to him but had adopted him? Would a birth certificate allay his fears? And what would bring on such fears in the first place? Was there a bit of craziness in every child that dissipated with the years, leaving, one hoped, a neurosis-free individual at maturity? "Try to remember, Rachel, even if it takes you a day or so. What could have made Susan doubt her parentage?"

"A day isn't going to do it. I think we were just playing once and she said, 'Did you ever think you might have been adopted?' and the truth is, I never did. But something made her think it was possible. And she came back to it. It worried her."

I threw out a far-fetched possibility. "Do you think she's gone off to find her real mother?"

There was a short silence. "If there's no real mother, how could she be looking for her?"

"I don't think this is a question of logic. Listen,

Rachel, if you think of anything, if you hear from Susan, please call me."

I hung up feeling very uncomfortable. This was not a topic I wanted to discuss with Ada Stark.

4

I went to the foot of the stairs and listened, but I could hear nothing. With the new addition on our house, already more than three months old but still new to me, our bedroom was no longer just a few feet from the staircase. It sat atop the new family room off the kitchen and was the most luxurious room I had ever called my own. I walked quietly up several steps till I heard the voice of my husband talking to our son. I smiled and listened for a few moments. They seemed to be having a fine time up there although the conversation was pretty one-sided. But as long as things were calm, I went back to the kitchen and looked at the brief list Ada had written for me.

The problem with the second person on the list, Jill Brady, was that all I had for her was her work number and today was Friday, the first of January. It wasn't likely she would be at her desk before Monday, and that was too far in the future to suit me. I took out our Manhattan directory and looked up Jill Brady. There was none listed. I tried Brooklyn with the same result, which didn't surprise me. Young single women often kept their names out of phone books to thwart nuisance calls or worse. Well, I had the business number and that seemed like the only place to start.

After one or two rings a thoroughly nonprofessional

male voice answered on a recording: "You have reached the offices of WJC. We are not open for business. Our regular office hours are Monday through Friday from nine A.M. to five-thirty P.M. If this is an emergency, please call . . ." and he dictated a number with a New Jersey area code, "and leave a message. We'll get back to you as soon as possible."

I took down the number, called it, and left a message that I hoped would encourage him to call back soon. I didn't have long to wait. The phone rang before I had a chance to do much else.

"Ms. Bennett?"

"Yes."

"This is W. J. Childs. You left a message about Susan Stark?"

"That's right. She hasn't been seen for the last two days and she missed some appointments. I'm trying to find Jill Brady to see if she knows anything that can help."

"I've got Jill's home number here somewhere. Hold on." He left the phone and I heard the sounds of a family, probably in another room. Then he came back and gave me the number.

"How long have you known Susan, Mr. Childs?"

" 'Bout a year. That's how long she's worked for me."

"How did you come to hire her?"

"Believe it or not, through an ad in the *New York Times*. I was starting up a new magazine and I needed a jack-of-all-trades, a writer, an editor, a researcher, someone in the right age group. I couldn't afford a whole staff so I hired Susan. She does a little of everything and she does it well."

"When did you last see her?"

"Uh, yesterday? No, must have been the day before. We took yesterday off. Have you talked to her boyfriend? I think they live together. He should know what's going on."

"I have," I said. "He picked her up at the office and he dropped her off in Brooklyn and no one's seen her since."

"Doesn't sound like Susan. She's a pretty together person."

"How did she seem the last time you saw her?"

"She seemed like Susan. I'm not the person to ask. I'm busy seventy minutes an hour, and I'm not known for noticing what people have on or if they've had a bad night."

"You knew Susan had a boyfriend."

"She introduced him at a party and I'm more or less aware they live together. Try Jill. She notices every time I wear a new tie to work. And their desks are near each others'. If Susan wanted to talk about herself, her problems, whatever, she'd probably talk to Jill."

OK, I thought. That's the next move.

"Could you say that again?" It was a girlish voice, confused but wide-awake.

"Mr. Childs gave me your home phone number. I'm Chris Bennett and I'm a friend of Susan Stark's mother. Susan hasn't been seen for two days and we're all very worried about her. I thought, since you know her from work, you might have some idea where to find her."

"I don't know where she went. She just said she'd need the car for most of the day."

"You lent her your car?"

"Yes. I didn't need it and it's better to give it a workout than let it sit for days on end. When you drive it, at least the battery gets charged up."

"When did you give it to her?"

"Well I gave her the keys on the thirtieth, two days

ago. I don't know if she was planning to use it that day or yesterday or both. She just said she had to drive somewhere and she was planning to rent a car and I said, 'Why don't you take mine?' "

"Has she returned the car, Jill?"

"I guess so. She said she would."

"You mean you haven't seen her?"

"She said she'd just put it back in my garage when she was through with it. I haven't looked because I don't need it. She'll give me the keys on Monday at work."

"Is your car far from where you live?"

"It's a couple of blocks. I rent the garage from an old couple with a house. They gave up their car a few years ago so they rent it out."

"Is it too far to walk to check whether Susan's brought it back?" I asked.

I heard her let out her breath. "I can go if it's really important. But it's getting dark and I think it's cold out."

"Call a taxi, Jill. I'll pay for it." It wasn't that I was feeling expansive; I just thought that if she refused, I'd have to let the police know, and they'd show up on her doorstep and ruin what was left of her day.

"Look, I'll walk over, OK? Give me your number and I'll call you back in an hour. I can't go just yet."

I dictated my number and told her to call collect. "Did Susan give you any hint of where she was going with the car?"

"She didn't say where, but she said she'd probably put a hundred miles or so on the car. Frankly, it sounded good to me. It's my father's old car and I keep having battery trouble in the winter. I really hate to drive in the ice and snow. I don't know what I keep it for. Between the garage and the insurance, I could rent a car cheaper."

"Thanks, Jill. You've really been a help. I'll be home all night, so whenever you call is fine."

I ran upstairs to tell the news to Jack.

"OK. That sounds like real progress. You know where that garage of Jill's is?"

"I forgot to ask but it's a 718 number, so it's Brooklyn or Queens."

"Or Staten Island," Jack said. "You remember the number?"

I remembered the first three digits.

"Brooklyn. So this Jill lives somewhere near the Starks, and Susan got dropped at the Starks' two days ago, and either went from there to the garage or slept over at the Starks' and picked up the car yesterday."

"And we'll find out in an hour or so if she returned it."

"If she didn't, we'll have to get the plate number and put it in the alarms."

"Jill's not going to like that."

"We've got a missing person and a lot of unanswered questions. This isn't a matter of liking it or not."

But I felt for Jill. She had done someone a kindness and accidentally got herself involved in a police inquiry. I hoped it wouldn't tear her life apart.

Jill called back as I was getting started on my busy hour with Eddie: his bath, his nursing, his nice, warm bed. The bath was almost ready when the phone rang.

"It's not there," Jill's voice said.

"The car hasn't been returned?"

"The garage is empty. I listened to my answering machine and she hasn't called. But I don't think there's anything to be alarmed about. She knew I wasn't going to use the car this weekend, and maybe she got back from wherever too late to drop it off yesterday, and today's a day for sleeping late. She probably left it in the street and she'll get it back tomorrow."

"Jill, can you give me the plate number on your car?"

"Why?" There was a note of hostility in the question.

"Because I think the police will want to keep an eye open for it."

"That's crazy. She didn't steal it. I lent it to her. I don't care whether it's back or not."

"But Susan's missing and she's very likely to be where the car is."

I could feel her distress in the silence. Then she dictated the plate number and described the car. It was an old maroon Chevy with a noticeable dent in the rear fender on the passenger side where, she explained sadly, a taxi had clipped her; her case was still pending.

I gave the information to Jack while I got Eddie ready for our big hour together, and he phoned it in to the Brooklyn precinct where he and Kevin had reported Susan's disappearance. Eddie had started to fill out into adorable chubbiness, and he had begun to smile regularly, making his parents about as happy as we had ever been. He had begun to love his bath, a distinct change from those first days home when he clearly hated it.

Clean, warm, and happy, he snuggled on my shoulder as I settled in an old rocker we had moved into his room. Jack came in as I was nursing and said there would be an alarm out for the car in the tri-state area.

"And they'll probably drop in on Jill Brady tonight, ask her the same questions you did, and get the same answers."

"I feel sorry for her, Jack. I start to see why people are reluctant to come forward."

"It has to be done, Chris. Boy, he's getting big, isn't he?"

I looked down at our son and brushed my fingers through his fine hair. "I guess there's no other way of conducting an investigation," I said with resignation.

"Gotta start somewhere."

"Let me give Arnold a quick call. Can you burp him?"

"Arnold?"

I giggled and handed Eddie over.

Arnold was home and came to the phone as soon as he heard Harriet mention my name. I briefed him, hearing his appreciative grunts as I went through what I had learned and from whom.

"I knew you'd be light-years ahead of the cops," he said. "It sounds like you've really learned something. But that bit about Susan thinking she's adopted. I've always thought she was a very sane girl, and that's crazy. I was there when Ada was pregnant and I was at the synagogue the night they named her. And I've never seen a mother and daughter look as much alike as those two."

"Arnold, forget the facts. Something was bothering her and that's how she made it real."

"You think she spent yesterday looking for a mythical birth mother?"

"I don't know, and she didn't tell anyone that I know where she was going, why, or what she expected to find."

"How far did she say she'd be driving?"

"About a hundred miles altogether. When Jack gets through burping Eddie, he'll drop a compass on a map and draw a circle with a radius of fifty miles. Let's see what we come up with."

"I don't think your compass is going to highlight any person or place that'll ring any bells. It's only an estimate anyway. And driving in circles never got me anywhere."

"I'm glad your sense of humor hasn't deserted you," I said.

"Was that my sense of humor talking? I thought it was my rational self. Well, maybe Harriet can scare up an old compass of our kids' and we'll draw our own circles. Where's ground zero? Brooklyn?"

"Somewhere near Ada Stark's house."

"Always knew Brooklyn was the center of the world. Thanks, Chrissie. You've restored my faith."

"In what?"

"In you. In the civilian population. In the ability of one smart human being with a telephone to dig up information."

I said my good-byes, retrieved my baby, and sat down in the rocker to finish what we had started.

5

Jack was working on our dinner when I got downstairs, stirring up something fragrantly mouth-watering in our electric frying pan. "You're right on time," he said. "Sit down and eat your grapefruit. This'll be ready in three minutes. Give or take."

He's very good at the "give or take." I've been cooking for myself, and for him, for two years now, and I'm still a wreck about when everything will be ready. For Jack there's just nothing to it. And since his sister is a caterer, I've come to believe it's in the blood or the genes or something I have no control over.

He sat down across from me and dug into his grapefruit. We had bought a carton of them from the glee club of the local high school, fund-raising for their annual trip. They were the best grapefruit we'd ever eaten, shipped up from Florida just before Thanksgiving, all pink and juicy. Next year we would buy two cartons and double our investment in the glee club.

Jack had also been busy with map and compass. "You get as far south as Trenton, New Jersey," he said, "halfway west across New Jersey, north about to Poughkeepsie, up to maybe Norwalk, Connecticut, halfway across Long Island, and out to sea if you're so inclined. All in a fifty-mile radius. We're within the radius, of course, but I don't think our lives intersect with Susan's. Or didn't until now."

"And if she was just estimating, it could have been forty or sixty one way."

"Right you are."

"So she went to see—or find—someone or something well outside the five boroughs, a trip she could easily make in one day even if it took as long as two hours to get there. And for some reason, she didn't come back," I said.

"Maybe she liked what she found."

"Then she should have made a phone call."

"Let me tell you about kids calling home. You know that wonderful mother of mine, the happiest grandmother in the world, the one who thinks you're the cat's meow? Do you know that when I was living in Brooklyn Heights maybe two miles from my folks—if you took the round-about way—and I went three days without checking in, she'd get on her high horse? You know how old I was?"

I had a good idea. "What you're saying is that parents get nervous when they don't hear from their kids and kids get resentful about calling home. What I'm saying is—"

"Susan should have called home. But the reason kids don't call home is that their parents make them crazy."

"What about Kevin? He's a lover, not a parent."

"You got me."

"And she borrowed a car," I persisted.

"And that's a friend, not a mother. You're right. I'm looking for reasons why we won't find a body."

It was the first time either of us had said it, and it gave me chills. "I think I'll call Rachel again after dinner. Now that we have some more information, maybe she can add to it." I cleared away the grapefruit halves and put the pasta on the table as Jack served the meat and vegetables.

"Suppose she went to see this possible natural mother of hers," he said.

"Jack, who would admit to such a thing if it weren't true?"

"Got me. Someone who could benefit from it."

"Who benefits from being somebody's natural mother?" I said it to myself. If you come out of the woodwork and identify yourself as my mother, what good does it do you?

"Eat. We'll think later."

Later I called Rachel and told her the story.

"She borrowed a car?" Rachel said, as though it were the last thing in the world anyone could borrow.

"From her friend at work."

"Why would she do that? Kevin has a car. She could have had his. She drives it all the time. She really must have wanted to keep whatever she was doing a secret from him."

"It does look that way, doesn't it?"

"And those places you mentioned. Trenton. Who would want to go to Trenton? Who would want to go to Norwalk?"

"They're just possibilities, Rachel, just places that are within a fifty-mile radius of Brooklyn. Did she ever talk to you about something or someone roughly that distance away?"

"She talked about Europe, about California. I think she and Kevin took a trip up to Canada last summer. She went to camp somewhere upstate, I think, when she was a kid. I didn't go but I wrote to her a couple of times. I can't remember the address. It was more than fifteen years ago."

"Did she talk about it? Did she have good memories of it?"

"She liked it. They had swimming and lots of arts and crafts."

I wondered whether I detected a bit of wistful envy in her voice. Her best friend had deserted her for a summer, for other friends and lots of activities you couldn't find on the streets of Brooklyn.

I decided to switch to something else that had occurred to me. "Did New Year's Eve have any significance in Susan's life?"

"Well you know, I think it did. Funny you should ask that."

"Tell me about it."

"Susan always felt—you know, when we were kids she read about how in the old days in China people settled their debts on New Year's Day. They forgave their debts, really. Started everything new for the new year. Susan loved that. If she'd had a fight with someone, she'd sit down on New Year's Eve and write them a letter. She always said she wanted to start the new year with a fresh slate."

"So she might have been settling some argument or problem yesterday," I said hopefully.

"It's possible. It's really possible."

"Help me figure out what it could be."

There was silence. "Nothing really pops into my head. I'll have to think about it, Chris. Have you asked Kevin?"

"Not yet."

"You should start there. You know, Susan and I are close, but when you take the big step, your whole life changes. She spent a lot more time with Kevin this past year than with me. If anything was bothering Susan, he would know about it."

I felt as though we'd been walking in a circle and had

just come back to our starting point. "She didn't borrow his car. She didn't want him to know where she was going."

"That's true. I don't know what to say."

"Just think about it. Maybe something will come to you." But I hung up feeling kind of down.

The truth is, I was exhausted. If I have inadvertently sounded like a supermom, it hasn't been intentional. For almost six weeks I had been working at being a good mother to my baby, but the lack of sleep had really taken its toll. When I thought about it, which I tried not to do very often, the most sleep I got at a stretch was a little more than three hours. I desperately wanted Eddie to sleep through his two A.M. feeding so I could put together a good seven hours for myself. Even six would do it. My pediatrician assured me that one night it would happen; I would just have to be patient.

Until now I had been able to grab an hour here or there during the day if I really needed it, since the class I teach was over for the first semester and would not resume for several weeks. But now there was Susan. If she were alive she had to be found, and much as I loved and admired my husband, much as I trusted in the ability of the police to come up with answers, this was too vague a problem for them to take very seriously. They would talk to Jill Brady tonight, but only because I had pointed them in that direction. A D.D.5 would find its way into the Susan Stark file with the particulars of the Brady interview. And then what? Would the file hold a series of D.D.5s leading to a closed case or the opening of a homicide investigation? It was up to those of us who cared to pick up the ball and run with it.

I wanted to talk to Susan's father but I wasn't sure he wanted to talk to me. I wanted Rachel to come up with something substantial to give us a direction. I wanted Jill Brady's car to be found with Susan at the wheel, alive and well and pooh-poohing all her family's worries. And I wanted to sleep through the night.

I didn't get any of my wishes. Eddie woke me at two and again at six and we got our day underway. It was Saturday, and happily for all of us, Jack was home for the weekend. At eight-thirty, I answered the phone to find my friend and neighbor Melanie Gross at the other end.

"Mel, it's so good to hear your voice. I feel like it's been weeks since we talked."

"Just days. How's it going? Eddie sleeping through the night yet?"

"Not yet. Dr. Schwartz said to be patient. I'm trying. But I'm really tired."

"Buck up. If I lived through it twice, you can. I have half the metabolism you have. There were days I didn't get dressed till five o'clock, and then only because some inner voice said I'd never make the Mommy Hall of Fame. Do you still have a sitter for when you go to see Dr. Campbell?"

Dr. Campbell was my obstetrician, recommended by Mel. "Yes, Elsie's on for that. I'll nurse him and drop him off."

"Chris," Mel said in her most authoritative tone of voice, "you can leave a bottle once in a while. I promise you nothing terrible will happen. And it will give you seven glorious hours to yourself."

"It certainly sounds inviting. And the way things are going, I'll probably be doing it sooner rather than later. A friend of Arnold Gold's disappeared the day before New Year's Eve and nobody's got any idea where she is." I filled her in briefly.

"I don't like the sound of it, Chris. A pretty, young

woman, alone somewhere in an old borrowed car that could have broken down. I get chills just thinking about it."

I hadn't really considered the possibility that the car had broken down, but remembering what Jill had said about the age of the car and the battery trouble she'd had, it could easily have happened. We talked for a while. Having a conversation on a topic other than babies and diets and doctors' appointments was absolutely invigorating. This dormant part of me was still there, awakening to the call. When I got off the phone, I may not have felt less tired, but I certainly felt more alive.

Jack and I breakfasted together, more or less like the old days. "I'm going to have to call Kevin again," I said, pouring more coffee for Jack while I stuck with skim milk. "He knew something was bothering Susan, but I'm not optimistic that he'll tell me any more than he did yesterday. If he even knows more."

"Want me to handle it?"

"On your weekend off?"

"Who's watching the clock?"

"I'd love it. You said you talked on your way to the precinct. Maybe if you can impress on him that strange things are going on—Susan borrowing a car so he wouldn't know she was going somewhere—he'll come around. Jack, how do we even know Kevin drove Susan to Brooklyn?"

"We don't. But if he didn't, what happened to Jill Brady's car?"

"Right. Good point."

"Unless, of course, he knew she was borrowing Jill's car and after he did something unspeakable to Susan, he did something else to the car."

"In which case we'll never get anything out of him."

"Let me give it a try."

"OK." I downed the remaining half glass of milk and

took a deep breath. I hadn't developed a taste for the stuff and I was pretty sure I wouldn't. "What I'll do is talk to Ada and see if she has any idea what there is in a fifty-mile radius that would draw Susan on the last day of the year. And try to talk to Susan's dad."

"Wasn't there another phone number on that list?"

I thought for a minute. "There was a third number, wasn't there?"

"A schoolteacher?"

"That's right. Mrs. Halliday." The memory returned. "You really think a teacher would know anything useful?"

"It's a lead. It's a phone call. I'd sure as hell make it if it were my case."

I looked at my watch. It was Saturday morning and I didn't want to bother anyone too early, but it seemed a decent time by now. I called the number Ada had given me.

A pleasant, older voice answered.

"Mrs. Halliday, my name is Christine Bennett. I'm a friend of Susan Stark's mother."

"Oh dear, is anything wrong?"

"No one's seen Susan since the thirtieth. She borrowed a car from a friend and said she'd be driving about fifty miles and back. Ada said you were a confidante of hers. Do you have any idea where she might have gone?"

"Well—"

I waited, suddenly filled with hope. She hadn't turned me down flatly with an I-haven't-the-faintest-idea kind of answer.

"I might actually be able to help you, but I'm not sure I should."

"I don't understand."

"Susan spoke to me in great confidence. It's always been that way. I would never want to betray that confidence."

"Mrs. Halliday, she told no one that she was going anywhere except the person she borrowed the car from, and she said the car would be back in its garage by New Year's Eve. It's not back yet and neither is Susan. Her family is very worried."

"Give me your name again and your number. I'll call Mrs. Stark and call you back."

It was a long wait, and I wondered whether she had changed her mind or failed to reach Ada or got stuck on a long phone call. I had my kitchen cleaned up by the time she called back.

"I'll talk to you, Miss Bennett. Chris, is it? But I can't do it over the phone and I can't promise to disclose everything that Susan has told me. I have an idea where you might look for her. How soon can you be here?"

This was it and I heard my heart thumping. "I have to feed my baby about ten o'clock," I said. "I should be ready to leave at eleven. Would twelve or twelve-fifteen be inconvenient?"

"It'll be fine. I'll open a can of tuna fish and we can lunch together."

"Tuna fish sounds great," I said. It was my staple for many years. "I'll see you then."

I had carefully not mentioned whether I was coming with or without my little Eddie, partly because I wasn't sure.

"Get her?" Jack asked, walking into the kitchen.

"Got her and she knows something. But I have to go down and see her in person."

"Great. Give me a little quality time alone with my son."

"You won't mind?" I asked, with all the hesitation I felt.

"I'll love it. Where are those emergency bottles we bought and never used?"

"Right here." I opened the cabinet.

"Terrific. Don't hurry back. I've got lots of things to talk to him about."

"You sure you can handle it?"

He gave me a hug and kiss. "You sure *you* can?"

The truth was, I wasn't.

6

So that was how I came to leave my house, my husband, and my baby behind, possibly to struggle through a first feeding without me. I promised myself I would not call to check up on them or rush home to make the two P.M. nursing. I was a woman of the world, I had a job to do, and I would do it. I drove down the street without looking back.

Mrs. Halliday lived in a different part of Brooklyn, in a much smaller house than the Starks'. It took a turn around the block before I found an empty space, and then a brisk walk in the cold took me to her house. The tiny patch of grass in front of it had long ago been replaced with concrete, which had lifted unevenly over the years, probably because of the roots of the single tree planted there. I went up the front walk and rang the bell.

"You must be Miss Bennett. Come in."

"Thank you. Please call me Chris. It's nice and warm in here."

"It's an old house, built like a fortress. Let me have your coat."

Mrs. Halliday wasn't what I expected. She was tall and fairly slim, wearing dark brown pants, a white blouse, and a tan suede vest. Her hair was cut short and was still in a state of flux, turning from dark to gray in a very attractive way. There was nothing "little" or "old" about her. I could imagine this woman having a job or catching the eye of a good-looking man.

"Lunch is on the table," she said, gesturing toward the kitchen. "I'm surprised to see you alone. I thought I'd have the pleasure of a baby's company."

I think I blushed a little. "I left him with his father. I'm not sure who's more nervous."

She smiled. "By the time you get home, no one will be nervous any more."

I liked her. The smile was genuine, the voice sincere. If she'd been my teacher when I was ten, I would have wanted to keep her forever as Susan had.

We sat down at the kitchen table where two salads were waiting for us. Each was garnished with half a hard-boiled egg, slices of cucumber, and some lettuce that wasn't iceberg. An array of salad dressings was clustered on the table and we each picked a different one.

"Where do you want me to begin?" my hostess asked, after offering me a choice of soft drinks.

"How did your friendship with Susan start?"

"She was my pupil when she was ten or eleven and I was correspondingly younger. She was a child of talent and depth and had great inner beauty. She was a little withdrawn perhaps, but with much inside that was trying to get out. She may have been overwhelmed by her parents, who are go-getters in their own right. Not that they neglected her; they didn't. She was brought up in a house full of love and has developed into a spectacular young woman."

"Do you know about her relationship with Kevin Angstrom?"

"Oh yes. We've talked about him."

"I haven't met her father," I said. "Do you know anything about him?"

"I probably haven't seen him since Susan was a pupil

of mine. She's very fond of him. I think he's a good man."

"And Mrs. Stark?"

"I talk to her from time to time. I think she's a good mother and a good person."

This was a woman of firm beliefs but I couldn't judge how accurate her appraisals were. Much of what she thought about Susan's parents could be a reflection of Susan's own feelings. I thought it was interesting that she had expressed no opinion whatever about Kevin, only admitting she knew about him.

"How often do you and Susan get together?" I asked.

"Very irregularly. I think Susan feels I'm a lonely, retired schoolteacher, but she's only half right. I retired a few years ago for a number of reasons we don't have to go into, and I work at another job a few days a week. I'm far from lonely, but I appreciate Susan's concern and I love seeing her. Whenever she drops by, I'm happy."

"Do you have a family, Mrs. Halliday?"

"I do. I was married years ago, widowed, but left with one daughter. I have no complaints."

"You said on the phone that you might be able to help me find Susan. I'd be very grateful for anything you can tell me."

"I had second thoughts after we spoke, but Mrs. Stark is really so upset at Susan's disappearance that I decided to tell you enough to give you a direction to move in. She seems to trust you, said you are a friend of an old friend."

"That's true."

"Are the police involved?"

"Minimally. Susan is an adult and she has a right to go where she pleases and not tell her family or her boyfriend. She borrowed someone's car and even though she hasn't returned it when she promised to, the owner of the car wasn't planning on using it this weekend anyway.

So it adds up to Susan missing a New Year's Eve party, returning a car late, and not calling home."

"I think you mentioned fifty miles?"

"She told the car's owner she might put a total of a hundred miles on the car."

"Well, that would certainly be the range."

"You know where she was going?"

"I know that Susan has been trying to find someone for many years. I can't tell you who the person is because it would cause a great deal of consternation in her family, and I don't know if this person even exists. But Susan believes that—" she paused, then said, "—this person exists." She didn't want to say "he" or "she."

"It's some time since I've seen Susan, a month or more," she continued. "She told me last time we spoke that she had a good lead, that the place was upstate, up the Hudson somewhere. Maybe your fifty miles would get you there."

"Do you have a name, a town, an address?"

"I do if I can coax it out of my mind."

I sat quietly while Mrs. Halliday closed her eyes. After a moment she pushed her chair back and stood, walked to the kitchen window, and looked out at the snowy back yard.

"Something like Blazerville," she said finally, and turned back to the window as though the inspiration might continue.

I wrote it down. The name didn't ring a bell. St. Stephen's Convent is "up the Hudson" and I've driven along both sides of the river for years.

"Blazertown?" she asked, as though I might have an answer.

"Now that I have a direction, I can look at a good map and find whichever town it is," I said. "Do you have a name for the person?"

"Susan never told me." She was facing me now, her back against the sink. "But it's an old farmhouse that no one's living in anymore. Except this person, of course."

"Do you have a street name, the name of a neighbor, anything that would get me closer than the town?"

"The name of the farmer. Remember the old song?" She sang, " 'Old MacDonald had a farm, Ee-i-ee-i-o.' It wasn't MacDonald but it was something like that. I can't remember much else. I only remember this 'Blazer' because she let it slip once. She never said it again. I've known for most of the years of our friendship that something was bothering Susan, that there was someone she needed to find. She said several times that her life was a jigsaw puzzle with one huge piece missing. That's the piece she's been searching for, but she's never come out and said something like, 'I'm going to meet Aunt Margaret if it's the last thing I do.' "

"Mrs. Halliday, I've been told by someone who knows Susan very well that she thinks she's adopted."

She smiled. "That's pretty foolish, isn't it?" she said.

"I think so. Her friend thinks so."

"So what is it that makes Susan believe that? That's what you should be asking."

"So you don't think she's off visiting her natural mother?"

"I think her natural mother lives with her natural father where Susan grew up. As to whom she's visiting, I don't really know, Chris, and anything I suspect I've gleaned from years of listening."

I heard her say "whom" and was reminded I was in the presence of a teacher, one old enough to make distinctions that my generation had all but abandoned. "Then she's never really told you?"

"Not in so many words."

"Do you think her mother would have any idea if I could think of a good way of putting it to her?"

"I think if you talk to Mrs. Stark about the possibility that Susan is adopted, she'll be very distressed, especially at this time. It will mean to her that her child missed something in their relationship. And I'm sure she feels that nothing is missing."

"From what I've heard, Susan has a very good relationship with her parents."

"I've heard the same. And I've heard it from Susan herself."

"I have a feeling I'm more confused now than when I came in."

"Why don't you just wait a day or so? Susan isn't expected back at work till Monday. Maybe she found this person and needs some time to think about things. Maybe she didn't find anyone, and that's given her more to think about. She borrowed a car, she said she was driving a hundred miles round-trip. She may just want to be alone for a day or two."

"She had a date with Kevin for New Year's Eve," I said.

"Ah yes, Kevin."

There it was again, the feeling that she was avoiding saying something negative. "Do you know much about him?"

"Only what Susan's told me. He sounds like a very nice young man. Perhaps 'young man' is a bit inaccurate. He's in his thirties, I believe."

"I think so. I met him yesterday. He seemed almost frantic at Susan's disappearance."

"Why didn't she tell him?" Mrs. Halliday mused. "They have a close relationship. I expect they'll marry. Is there something about him that kept her from telling him her secret?"

"Why didn't she tell you?" I countered.

"You're right to ask. In many ways I'm the perfect person for her to have told. I'm not family. I'm not judgmental. I love her dearly."

It was a question I would ask myself.

I walked through the cold to my car. It was too late to attempt to get home for Eddie's two-ish nursing, and although I was still nervous about leaving father and son alone, another part of me was glad. I would take my time, stop to do some shopping on the way. I had witnessed Dr. Campbell cutting the physical cord; now I would take Step Number One toward cutting the deeper, emotional one that bound me to my sweet infant son. I had the sense that something momentous was happening, something only I was aware of in this great world where people were going their own ways on a sunny winter Saturday. I passed a woman with two young children, one in a stroller. Had she been as affected as I the first time she left them? I waved to the little girl, the older one, and she smiled and waved back. I pulled my keys out and let myself into my car. I was a wife, a mother, and a free woman. I felt very good about all three.

I thought about Mrs. Halliday on the way home. She probably knew or suspected more than she had told me but unless there was an indication of foul play, it wasn't likely she would open up further. I had a direction, a possible town, the name of a farmer—although I didn't quite understand what role he played in all this. Jack would help me find the town and a phone book might do the rest.

I got home a little after four with a bag of groceries. I went around to the front of the house to check on the mail and let myself into the living room through the front door. Since we built the addition, we don't use the living room much. There wasn't a sound, so I kept quiet. I hung up my coat, dropped the bag in the kitchen, and went on to the family room, which is a couple of steps down from the kitchen. It was perfectly silent and I looked around, seeing my husband stretched out on the leather sofa, fast asleep. A little sound made me turn my head. Eddie was sitting in his baby chair on the floor near the sofa. I walked toward him, and he gave me the biggest smile of his life.

"Hi, little sweetheart," I said with absolute joy. "You recognize me, don't you? It's Mommy."

The smile lingered and he moved his arms and legs as I bent to pick him up.

"Chris?" Jack's sleepy voice said.

"He knows me, Jack," I said. "Look how happy he is to see me."

"Oh boy. I must've dropped off."

I sat down next to Jack with Eddie on my lap. His little hands were waving. "Did Daddy take good care of you?" I asked.

"He ate like a horse, burped like a champ, slept for an hour, and then I couldn't keep him quiet. He wore me out."

"Go back to sleep, honey. I'll keep him company."

"Were you worried?"

"Me? I knew I'd left him in good hands."

"I mean about me. This was a first, you know?"

I took a deep breath. "I knew you could handle it." Then I sat back and relaxed.

7

After I put Eddie to bed Jack filled me in on his day. While I was out Jill had telephoned to say the police had come to interview her last night, and she hadn't sounded happy about it. She wished people would just leave her alone.

Then Jack had called the detective who caught the case and he had said words to the effect that, hey, a gal borrows a car, says she's taking a hundred-mile drive, and she knows the car doesn't have to be back till Sunday night. What's the problem?

The problem was, she hadn't called home and had missed a big date, but the detective didn't seem to think much of that. You never knew a girl who took longer getting home than she said?

"So then I called Kevin," Jack went on. "That wasn't just a zero; it was a minus. If you want my opinion, he doesn't know the first thing about what's going on in Susan's head. He doesn't know where she went or why. He knows something's bothering her but she's never let him in on her secret. And it really gripes him to have to admit it."

"Even to a nice guy like you."

"Even that. So where are you?"

I told him what I'd learned from Mrs. Halliday.

"Looks like you're light-years ahead of anyone else. Let me have a look at the map."

He left the family room and went upstairs to where such things are filed away, or at least stacked. When he came back, he was already scrutinizing a map. "Maybe it's too small to be listed. I'll call the Six Five and see if anyone there can help me." The Six Five is his precinct in Brooklyn.

I looked at the map while he went to the kitchen to make the call. I had turned down his suggestion of a telephone in this room or of a portable phone. It was less than two and a half years since I had left the spare and frugal life of a nun, and something in me rebelled at filling my life and my home with the kinds of extras I saw on the small screen all the time. We had a huge family room now, where a beautiful fire was burning in our magnificent fireplace (that I had argued against but gladly lost that battle), surrounded by new furniture that I had been sure we could do without. A few steps into the kitchen to make a call or answer the phone would do neither of us any harm.

"Got it!" Jack said triumphantly, as he came back. "How does Bladesville grab you?"

"Sounds good. How far is it from Brooklyn?"

"Within the fifty-miles-give-or-take range. I've got the number of the local sheriff's office and the nearest state trooper barracks. It's too small a town to make the map of New York State. Shall I give them a call and ask for the address of Old MacDonald?"

"Absolutely." I got up and stood at the steps to the kitchen to listen to the call. This was cop-to-cop talk and it went smoothly, with Jack doing a lot of writing and uh-huh-ing. When he hung up, he looked happy.

"Even got you driving instructions," he said. We went

back to our warm seats near the fire. "It's not Old Mac-Donald. It's Fred Donaldson."

"Close enough. What's the story?"

"Farmer Donaldson is retired, sold off part of his land a couple of years ago, but kept the part with the old farmhouse, not for sentimental reasons, according to Deputy Gridley, but because it's less desirable for builders."

"They're putting up split-levels in Bladesville?"

"Sounds like it. And it sounds like he's your guy."

"It sure does. I hope he hasn't gone south for the winter."

"I'll give him a call."

I could see that Jack was enjoying this. And I was glad he was making the calls. I'm still not happy talking to strangers on the phone.

I listened as he obviously spoke to the farmer himself, making up a story that he might be interested in the real estate. That, I thought, would keep him at home even if it made my appearance at his door a little suspicious. Personally, I hate making up stories although I know it's done all the time.

"He'll be there tomorrow," Jack said. "Wasn't planning on going anywhere. You up for a trip?"

"I think I have to make it. What about you?"

"I'll baby-sit. I've got a lot of reading to do."

"What do I do if the worst happens?" I was sure he'd know what I meant.

"Just back out of there and head for the nearest sheriff's office or substation. Don't touch anything, don't move anything. No heroics, OK? And have them call me so I can get you home in time for the next feeding." He leaned over and patted my hand. "You'll know when you walk in—if the door is unlocked and no one answers. You'll smell it. If someone died in there three days earlier, you'll know right away. Just get out and either report it, or come home and I'll make the call."

I didn't have to tell him I was scared.

We talked about whether or not to call Arnold or Ada Stark and decided against it. If Susan had surfaced, we would have heard. There was no reason to alert or alarm anyone. By tomorrow evening I might well know a lot more, and I would pass it along.

I got the laundry going and made some formula for Jack to use. When Eddie got up for his ten o'clock, I was ready for him and ready for bed. I was asleep minutes after my son.

I slept like a log. When the little cry awoke me in the dark, I felt curiously refreshed. I glanced at the clock on my night table. It was a quarter to six. Eddie had slept through the night!

I went to early mass and dropped in to visit my cousin Gene, who lives at Greenwillow, the home for adults with retardation several blocks from our house. I told him that as soon as I could, I would have him over for dinner and to see the baby. The idea of my having a baby confused him, but he has a very sweet disposition and he appeared to accept it. He had seen Eddie only once, at the baptism at Jack's family church in Brooklyn. Now it was time to have him see Eddie in the house where they could get to know each other, but I would have to let it go another week.

I got home in time for the late-morning nursing, after which Eddie very cooperatively fell asleep. I told Jack I would be back in seven hours or less—I was hoping for much less—and he gave me some last-minute suggestions and a kiss. I took the map, the directions, the names, and the addresses, got one more kiss, and set out.

* * *

Since we live northeast of Brooklyn, on the north shore of Long Island Sound, my trip was considerably shorter than Susan Stark's had been, if indeed she made this trip. I was able to drive slightly west and then pick up the road north along the Hudson. Farmer Fred Donaldson wasn't living in Bladesville anymore; he had moved to a nearby town, and I drove there first since Jack hadn't been able to get the farmhouse address from the deputy sheriff.

Mr. Donaldson had traded in a farm and a farmhouse for a neat one-story house on perhaps half an acre, the kind that might be built on the land he had sold. His front lawn was covered with snow but his walk was shoveled, as was the driveway to the two-car garage. I parked in front and walked to the door.

A lean man with weather-beaten skin opened the door at my ring. "Help ya?" he asked.

"I hope so. I'm Chris Bennett and I'm looking for a young woman who may be living in your farmhouse."

"Don't have a farmhouse."

"I thought—"

"You lookin' to buy a piece of property?"

"No, I'm looking for a—"

"Can't help ya."

"Mr. Donaldson, it's very important that I find this person."

"You the folks who called last night?"

"I didn't call," I said, speaking the truth in a narrow sense.

He considered for a moment. "What do you want this girl for?"

"Her mother's looking for her. Her fiancé is looking for her."

"You her sister?"

"No. I'm her friend."

"Step inside. It's cold out there."

I walked into a small foyer in a very warm house. "I'd like to know the address of the farmhouse so I can run over and talk to her."

"What's her name?" the farmer asked.

"Susan Stark."

"Ain't the name she gave me."

"What name did she give you?" At least he had admitted there was a female living at the house.

"Sally Smith or some such nonsense. Took me for a fool. No ID, no nothin'. Said she needed a place to live for a while, said she'd pay cash in advance."

I opened my bag and found the photo Ada had given me. "Is this the person?"

He took it in his hand and held it at arm's length. "Maybe yes. Maybe no," he said without conviction. He turned away. "Mother, come here," he called.

A woman about his age came in, carrying a dish towel. She smiled at me and we exchanged hellos.

"This the gal who rented the farmhouse?"

She was wearing glasses and held the picture close to her face. "That's her. Different clothes, but that's her."

"What was she wearing?" I asked, although it didn't make much difference.

"Oh, blue jeans, I guess. Big, heavy shoes."

"Hair's different," her husband said.

"Girls change their hair, Fred. Don't make 'em different people."

"Suit yourself."

"When did she come to you?" I asked.

"Five, six months ago. Paid for six months. Time's up end of February." He pronounced it without the first *r*.

So she must have seen the house in July. "How did she happen to come to you for a place to live?"

"Said she had a friend lived somewheres around here. Never said who the friend was. You ain't from the police, are you?"

"Not at all. Why?"

"Fred," his wife said, "leave it be."

"No one's supposed to live there," he said, as his wife frowned. "It's a hazard." He said the word sarcastically, implying it had been a decision made by someone else.

"Could you tell me how to get there?" I asked, reaching into my bag for a pen and paper.

He spelled out the route with his wife making critical comments as he went along: That road wasn't likely to be plowed, shouldn't you tell the lady to go the other way round? I hoped there would be someone along the road who could help me if I needed it. When I had the best of their combined directions, I thanked them and went out to my car.

It was still a bit of a trip to Bladesville, a town you could easily miss if your attention wandered. I drove past the little grocery store that looked like a relic of another century and made a left turn at the next corner. Probably there was a mall nearby where people went to buy their weekly necessities, and the little store I had just passed existed because people have food emergencies and cravings.

The road began to slope uphill, as I had been warned, and I slowed to make sure I didn't skid. Somewhere ahead there would be a right turn and then I would be on the road Mrs. Donaldson had thought I might better approach from the other direction. I hoped I wouldn't have to turn around and start over. And I wondered, as I drove slowly, keeping my eye out for the turn, how many people would be willing to buy split-levels quite this far from the center of town and whether this road could be kept free enough of snow that a school bus could drive on it safely in a bad winter.

I saw the right turn coming and cornered smoothly. The road had indeed been plowed, just wide enough for a single car to pass, but I didn't worry much that I would encounter traffic. I passed one working farm, a four-wheel drive parked up near the house and signs of life like chimney smoke. It was a big farm, the fields covered with snow and the barns in good shape.

And then I saw it, a weathered, shabby house, a faded red barn half fallen down. I slowed, looking for a driveway. I saw tire tracks and I turned onto the property, following them. There was no mailbox at the road, no smoke, no visible car. I drove as close to the house as I dared. The car had good radials, courtesy of Jack, but I didn't want to put them to the test.

"Well, this is it," I said aloud. I took my handbag for no reason and got out of the car. The snow crunched beneath my boots; the wind blew cold and stirred it up into a flurry. I was scared. Everything that had happened since New Year's Eve had led me to this lonely place, this falling-down barn and sad-looking house.

I went to the door and pressed the bell. There was no sound, and for the first time it occurred to me there might be no electricity inside. How could she live in a house with no light, no heat, perhaps even no water? And why would she want to?

I knocked, pressed my ear to the door, and heard nothing. "Susan?" I called. "Anybody home?"

Nothing. I walked to my left to the first window, but it was curtained and I couldn't see inside. So was the next one, and the next. I went back to the center of the front porch and down the stairs, then to the side of the house and along it. Some windows had shades drawn; some looked as though sheets had been stretched across them. I continued along, pressing through high snow, circling the house, calling as much to hear the sound of my own voice as to alert anyone inside.

There was a back door but it, too, yielded no results. I turned the knob and pushed, but it was locked. I kept going, looking for a car, a truck, any kind of transportation, but there wasn't even a tire track back here. Finally, I completed my circle and went up the stairs to the front porch.

I knew what I had to do. I had to turn the knob and push the front door to see if it was open. Either that or I had to find the sheriff's department and ask them to do it, making a fool of myself if they came up here and found the door unlocked. You dragged us up here to turn a doorknob? Well, probably a little more polite than that, but embarrassing nevertheless.

I called Susan's name one last time. I knew there was no one in there, no one who could hear me. I grasped the knob and turned, then pushed the door. It opened easily.

"Susan?" I called, my voice a little less strong, a lot less certain. "Anyone home?"

There was no smell but there was no heat either, and it was cold enough that a body could be well preserved. I pulled the door shut and backed away.

8

The little restaurant seemed the likeliest place to find a phone and have a chance to sit and munch on something. I didn't count on having every pair of eyes turn to me as I walked inside, but I ignored them and went over to the pay phone, not far from the cashier's station and within hearing of almost everyone sitting at a table.

I cracked open a fresh roll of quarters and dialed the familiar number of St. Stephen's convent. The woman who answered wasn't my friend Angela, who was probably off today, but a nun from the Villa, the home of the older, retired nuns. I took a minute to be sociable—it wasn't her fault I was a nervous wreck—and then asked for Sister Joseph, my closest friend and the General Superior of the convent.

A moment later I heard her calm, reassuring voice. "Chris, how good to hear from you. How's our baby?"

"Fat and happy and smiling."

"That's wonderful. Will you be bringing him up here for a visit?"

"In a couple of weeks. Joseph, I have a favor to ask of you. It's quite urgent."

"Yes, of course. Go on."

"I'm at a pay phone and I think everyone in this little restaurant is watching me. Do you know Bladesville?"

"I've driven through it once or twice. It's an hour from here, I would think."

"Can you meet me in the Bladesville Family Restaurant?"

"As soon as I can."

I was saying, "Thank you," when she hung up.

I took my coat and hat off and sat at a table as far from other people as I could manage. Now that I knew Joseph was on her way, I recognized that I was hungry. The sole waitress came over to my table, greeted me, and handed me a menu with far too many choices for my diminished attention span.

"We have a few specials," she said. "A salad plate with tuna, shrimp, and egg, a—"

"That sounds great," I said, the word tuna making my decision for me.

"And to drink?"

"A glass of milk. Skim if you have it."

"I think we do. Be right back."

I wasn't in a hurry. I checked my watch again and sat back. I hadn't thought to bring a book along, hadn't imagined there would be time to read. I was sorry I hadn't taken at least a section or two of the *Times*. I took out my notebook and opened it. There were all my notes from conversations with Kevin and Ada and Rachel and Jill and Mrs. Halliday. I could see how one piece of information led to another, how I had ended up in Bladesville, a town I hadn't heard of three days ago when Susan became a missing person to those closest to her.

I made some notes from memory on my conversation with the Donaldsons. Susan had turned up five or six months ago, her hair was different from the picture, she wore heavy shoes. A friend in the area had mentioned the farm to her.

"There you go." The waitress set down a beautiful salad, a roll and butter, a glass of skim milk.

I set aside the notebook and started to eat. I hadn't realized how hungry I was. The food was really very good and I ate it slowly, knowing that I was now enjoying the best part of the day.

"You look marvelous." We hugged and Joseph slid into the chair next to mine. "I see why you were so secretive on the phone. You were practically addressing everyone here."

"Thanks so much for coming. I'm in the midst of a search for a missing young woman and I can't take the next step alone." I filled her in, and she agreed we were better off going into the house together. I had already paid my bill so we went outside, hopped into my car, and drove back to the Donaldson farm.

"It's certainly away from the crowds," Joseph said, as we got out of the car. "Do you have any idea why she would want to spend time here?"

"No idea that makes any sense. I'm glad you thought to wear boots."

"Well you can't go far from the Mother House without them. Harold's busy getting the walks clear. Classes start again tomorrow, and the students will be coming back today."

The college is on the convent grounds, a small liberal arts school where I taught English for a number of years as a nun. "I don't think anyone's plowed here for a long time. There were tire tracks before I came so I assumed that was the driveway. But there's no car anywhere that I could see."

Joseph looked around. "Might be one in that old barn."

We walked up the steps to the front porch. "Ready?" I asked.

"Go ahead."

I opened the door and we stepped in. I called a couple of times but there was no answer, no sound of any kind. "This must have been the living room," I said as we entered a large room to the left of the door. Most of the furniture was gone, probably moved to the Donaldsons' new home, but a few old pieces were arranged rather haphazardly on the bare, dusty floor.

Joseph walked back to the dining room. "Nothing here either," she called. "Just an old chandelier that's seen better days."

I followed her and looked around the bare room. I could see where a rug had covered a rectangle on the floor; the wood was two distinct shades of brown, the outer rectangle bleached. I glanced around. Joseph was gone.

"Don't come in here, Chris." Joseph's voice came from somewhere beyond the dining room.

Cold as it was, I felt a chill. "What is it?"

"I think I've found her."

"Oh, God."

Joseph appeared in the doorway, her face pale. She put her hand on the wall. "It looks as though she was bludgeoned."

"Oh, Joseph." I went over to her. "I think I need to take a look. Stay here."

Her color had come back and she followed me into the kitchen. The body lay sprawled face-down on the floor on the left side of the kitchen among overturned chairs, broken dishes, a couple of pots and pans—indications that the poor victim had not accepted her fate without a fight. Blood was splattered on the walls and had run across the floor in thin streams, where it had frozen in ugly reddish-brown, three-dimensional trails.

What little skin that wasn't hidden by her hair had a

grayish pallor. One hand was beneath her, the other extended, its color a bluish-black that made me shiver.

On the right side of the room near the outside wall, about halfway into the kitchen, was a tall cast-iron wood-stove with a tubular chimney that rose vertically, then made a sharp right turn and went through the wall, a pretty reliable source of heat if you had wood to feed it. And against the wall near it was a makeshift bed, a pillow, and blankets and flannel sheets that might or might not have covered a thin mattress. When the weather had gotten cold, Susan had moved into the kitchen. I knew better than to disturb a crime scene, but I made my way carefully to the stove and touched it.

"Ice cold," I said.

"Not surprising. It's almost as cold in here as outside. You just don't feel the wind. I don't know how they'll determine when she died."

"She came up here three days ago. She was looking for someone or going to meet someone."

"It looks like she found him. Or he found her."

"Joseph, before I report this to the police, I want to take a look around the house. Even if they find anything, they'll never tell me and I know enough not to disturb what's here."

"Let's go to it."

I took a last look around the kitchen. On the table where she had had her last meal was an ancient manual typewriter with no paper in it. I didn't see anything that looked like a suitcase or a knapsack or a woman's handbag. On a small table near the door there were some pens and pencils but no paper, no newspaper, no letters. I led the way out of the room.

We went upstairs where there were several bedrooms, most of them empty, and a bathroom that would have been harboring the worst of the microscopic world if it hadn't been so cold. One bedroom had obviously been Susan's. There was a bed now stripped of its mattress and blankets, an old dresser that had some clothes in it but nothing else, a closet with a few wire hangers on a rod and some old shoe boxes, all empty, on the floor among assorted scraps of tissue paper and brown wrapping paper.

"Just some socks and underwear in the dresser," I said. "No letters or papers."

"She must have moved most of her things downstairs."

"If there was anything else. She couldn't have spent a lot of time here. She had a job, a boyfriend, family and friends."

"Perhaps it was a weekend retreat," Joseph said.

"But why?"

"That's what you'll have to find out. That's what will lead you to her killer."

We went back downstairs and looked around the living room and dining room again. Even the coat closet near the door was empty. I went back to the kitchen and looked around. A down jacket was lying on the floor near the makeshift bed. I stepped carefully over rivulets of blood and reached for it.

There were gloves in the pockets, a dirty tissue, and a few coins. The gloves were gray knitted wool, the index finger of the right hand starting to fray at the tip. "Right-handed," I said. "Do you see a wallet or purse anywhere, Joseph?"

"I've been looking for that but I haven't found any. The killer must have taken it with him."

"To make it look like a burglary."

"Or to keep us from confirming her identity. The killer may have thought she wouldn't be found till spring and by then no one would be able to identify her."

"No one can identify her now with her head bashed in

that way. Well, maybe her face was spared." I made my way carefully back to the doorway. I was thinking that if they wanted to compare fingerprints, Ada and I had all but obliterated them from Susan's desk. Perhaps there were things in Kevin's apartment that hadn't yet been polished away by a zealous housekeeper.

We left the house without saying anything. In the car, I thanked her for coming. "I couldn't do it myself."

"You knew she was in there dead."

"I suspected it. I had terrible feelings about this."

"It's better to know, Chris. It's better than not knowing."

I backed out and turned onto the road. "But her mother," I said. "How am I going to tell her mother?"

Bladesville shared a sheriff's department with the next town. They took us back to the farmhouse in a deputy's car, two brown-uniformed deputies, neither of whom wanted to be the only one to go into the house any more than I had, although one of them was old enough to have seen some bodies in his career. They left us in the car with the motor running as they went in. They didn't stay long; they came out looking pretty grim and a lot grayer than when they went in. The older of the two, Sergeant Holzer, called the county police from the car. Then he drove us back to the sheriff's office and took our statements.

It took a long time because there were a lot of calls to be made, to the local coroner, to a county detective who was attending a wedding somewhere and would have his Sunday ruined, to poor Farmer Donaldson who would rue the day he opened his door to me. He had rented the farmhouse illegally. The property had been condemned because of safety hazards and was, in the opinion of the local building inspector, likely to fall down at any moment.

I was asked, of course, how I happened to be at the farmhouse, who I was looking for, who had put me onto the Bladesville address, and so on. I gave the deputy the name and phone number of the Brooklyn detective whose case it was, and he, of course, was off on Sunday and apparently not carrying a beeper wherever he was spending his afternoon. Frustrated, the deputy spent time on the phone talking to someone else who read from the file and said it would be faxed over later when the fax machine was free.

Someone else interviewed Joseph, who had very little to say but left her interviewer looking rather uneasy. She was wearing the brown habit of the Franciscan order, and I heard the officer assure her he was a good Catholic and very sorry to be taking her time. I smiled at his discomfort. He was probably remembering some terrible incident from his rambunctious childhood when he had felt put upon by a nun in his classroom.

It was finally over, and Joseph and I spent a little time together talking before we went off in opposite directions. I tried to reach Arnold but no one answered. I had just about enough time to get myself back to Oakwood and bathe and nurse my lovely baby, so I went out to the car and started for home. The worst had happened, and I hoped the police would be inspired to get to work now even though it was too late to find Susan alive.

9

"Glad you made it," Jack said as I came inside the house. "I was starting to worry."

"We found her dead," I said, taking my coat off quickly. There was a lot to do.

"We?"

"I called Joseph when I found the door open."

"So the worst happened." He took my coat and hung it in the closet as I ran to find Eddie. He was crying in the family room, hungry, tired, ready for his evening attention.

I had very little free time for the next hour, but Jack called the precinct and asked that no one notify Susan's parents and boyfriend until we had made the first call. Whoever he spoke to wasn't sorry to give up that most unpleasant part of his duties.

Jack had something in the oven when I came home, and when I finally put Eddie to bed about an hour and a half after walking into the house, we sat down to one of his great meals, roast beef with real Yorkshire pudding. I was so hungry I gobbled it up, hardly uttering a word till I was through.

"I'm glad Sister Joseph came to help. You could have called the police, you know."

"I kept thinking there'd be nothing in the house, I'd get Farmer Donaldson in trouble for illegally renting the house—which I did—and they'd think I was nuts. Joseph drove over and we went inside together."

"It must have looked pretty terrible."

"It did, but there wasn't any smell. There was no heat and the body was frozen."

"So there wasn't much deterioration."

"I couldn't really tell. She was lying face-down so all I saw was one bluish-black hand, her jeans, her sweater, and her hair. Someone bashed her head in. I hope there's enough of a face left for identification."

"There are other means," Jack said. "By the way, Melanie brought over some cookies."

"Bless her heart. Where does she get the time now that she's teaching?"

"She said she just got going this afternoon and never stopped. We should have them over one of these evenings, Chris. I think you two miss each other, and I always enjoy talking to Hal."

"She'll need a sitter," I reminded him.

"You're right. I forgot."

We had usually gone over to the Grosses'. It was so easy, just lock the front door and walk down the street. "I'll talk to her. You're right, I really miss her. I haven't been walking in the morning since Eddie came." Mel and I had met during our morning outings over two years ago.

"You'll walk in the spring."

"I've got to call Arnold, Jack. I think he's the best person to talk to the Starks. The cookies'll have to wait."

"You think walking in on the body is the hard part," he said solemnly. "Then you start making the phone calls and find out what's really tough."

He was right. I went to the phone with a heavy heart.

* * *

"You found her body?" Arnold said, full of disbelief.

"Yes. I'm sorry. It was in a farmhouse up the Hudson."

"This is terrible. I don't know how this could have happened. How did you come to this place, Chris?"

"I had a conversation with Susan's old schoolteacher. Susan told her things, private things, that she doesn't seem to have told anyone else. What she told me fitted right in with what the owner of the car Susan borrowed said, that wherever Susan was going, it was about fifty miles from Brooklyn. I followed up on it and found the farmhouse. Sister Joseph drove over to go inside the house with me. I couldn't do it alone." Arnold knew Joseph, having met her—and talked to her with great pleasure and admiration—at our wedding.

"Have the Starks been notified?"

"Jack asked the police to hold off. Would you like me to do it?"

"I'd like anyone in the world to do it, but I think it's my duty as a friend."

"I'm so sorry, Arnold."

"Did you find the car up there?"

"I didn't see it on the property. There's a chance it's in one of the farm buildings."

"Thanks, Chris. We'll talk."

I didn't envy him the next ten minutes of his life.

We talked about it as we ate Melanie's wonderful cookies.

"She had a secret life, Chris," Jack said. "She may have been involved in something sordid or illegal, and whatever it was she handled it from that house upstate."

"You're thinking drugs?"

"Could be. Doesn't have to be. Maybe it was a relationship. How did she find that place anyhow?"

"The farmer said someone she knew up there told her the house was empty."

"That's a lot of doors to knock on," he said, thinking like a cop. "Everyone in Bladesville and all the surrounding towns."

"You mean someone she knows steers her to a lonely farmhouse and then kills her?"

"It's an idea. If you hadn't hit on that schoolteacher, no one would have found her till the farmer started showing prospective buyers the house. It could have been a long time."

That was true. The better portion of the property had been sold; the farmhouse was certified unlivable. "And by the time they found her, no one would even associate her body with a missing Brooklyn girl."

"That's probably how he looked at it. Not a perfect crime, but damn close."

"But it didn't happen that way, Jack. He didn't count on my talking to Mrs. Halliday and finding the body three days after the murder. I think the police have a pretty good chance at this one."

"Let's hope so."

Arnold called about nine o'clock. "This has to be one of the worst days of my life," he said, sounding far from his usual chipper self. "They've typed the blood and it's Susan's. Ada and Ernie are looking around for things in the house that might have Susan's prints on them."

"Kevin's apartment might be a better place to look. Has he been notified?"

"Yes. I called him myself. He's as broken up as Ada and Ernie."

Or a good actor, I thought uncharitably. "Arnold, does anyone have any idea what Susan wanted a lonely farmhouse for? She rented it five months ago and paid for six months in cash."

"Well, I certainly don't know. Maybe Kevin does but he's not talking, and I can't get anything out of Ada and Ernie now, I'm sure you understand why. And I think they're finding this as mysterious and unexplainable as I am."

"She has some connection up there, Arnold, a friend who lives around there and knew about the empty farmhouse. Now that's not just a person who drives down that road. It's someone who knows the area."

"I'm sure you're right, Chrissie, but my brain won't take any more of this today. And believe it or not, I have to be in court first thing tomorrow morning."

"OK. We'll talk another day. Let me know if anything turns up."

Monday was back-to-work day. Jack was off to Brooklyn to the Six Five and Mel was off to the town school where she had a one-year appointment. I was going back to teaching at a local college, but happily, I didn't have to think about that for a couple of weeks. My teaching consisted of one course that met on Tuesday mornings, and my mother's old friend Elsie Rivers had promised long ago to baby-sit. It was an ideal arrangement. She was trustworthy and grandmotherly and close by. Tomorrow, when I went to my obstetrician for my six-week checkup, I would drop Eddie off for the first time and see how everything worked out. I was sure it would go well.

But today it was just the two of us, with perhaps a late afternoon visit from Mel. Jack wouldn't be home for dinner because his evening law school classes were resuming, and that meant returning to the late nights we had grown accustomed to since shortly after we had met. I got the house in shape, checked with Elsie about tomorrow, took Eddie out for a walk in the cold winter air, and, after his two o'clock feeding, lay down for a well-needed nap. I was awakened after three by the telephone. It was Arnold.

"The coroner upstate decided not to ask the Starks to identify the body," he said. "There isn't much of a face left."

"I was afraid of that."

"So they'll try for prints. Kevin had a bunch of things he was sure she had held, so they're using those to find a match."

"What about DNA?"

"Takes a long time but they may do it anyway. If they can match prints, that's good enough. They've already got the right blood type. Ada doesn't have the faintest idea who Susan might have known up in that part of New York State. Neither does Kevin."

"Arnold, Kevin knows that something was bothering Susan and he won't talk about it. But he might know more than he lets on."

"I'll pass that along."

"Do the police have any leads?" I asked.

"Not that I've heard. I'm afraid you and the deputies up there did a great job of obliterating any tire tracks."

"I thought of that when it was too late."

"Well, don't worry about it."

"Do you want me to keep working on this, Arnold? I can leave Eddie for several hours at a time."

"Let's wait and see what the sheriff comes up with."

For the moment that seemed the best way to go. I had a doctor's appointment tomorrow, which would keep me in the area but wouldn't stop me from thinking. Very little stops me from thinking besides fatigue. I wanted to come up with a lead to the person who had told Susan about the Donaldson farmhouse. If she had a relative in the Bladesville area, her parents would know. If there were a friend that she talked about, Kevin would know. Unless Kevin himself were the friend.

Mel and her kids dropped over after four, and we all sat in the family room while the adults talked and the two school-aged children played. I had picked up some toys recently so they wouldn't be bored to tears when they visited, and their newness seemed to keep them happily occupied. I was learning pretty quickly that there was more to being a mother than caring for a baby.

"The cookies are great," I told Mel.

"I made a million of them, but there's only half a million left twenty-four hours later. I really love being back in the classroom, but I hate the idea of living out of the microwave."

"I can understand that. Especially since your home-cooked food is super-good."

"But you know, I've lost some weight since I started to teach. There aren't as many sweets in the house to nibble on. All those years of running and what finally took the pounds off was going back to work!"

"I just hope not taking my morning walk won't affect me the other way."

"You were born thin, Chris," Mel said, with a sigh. "And I wasn't. Tell me about your trip upstate."

I had told her the essence of it over the phone, which was half the reason she was here. Now I told her the rest and finished by saying how much I would like to figure out who had suggested the farmhouse to Susan.

"Maybe a retired teacher," Mel said. "She had a good relationship with one. Maybe she had a good relationship with another."

"OK, that's something to think about. Keep talking. You've already got one idea more than I have."

"There's always an old boyfriend. Her mother might remember a name for you."

"Why would a young person want to live in a village of five hundred or so up the Hudson, away from the big city and all his friends?"

"Maybe there's a commune up there. And you know, a lot of young families have turned to farming to get away from the big city and return to the earth."

"I hadn't thought of that."

"Or maybe he's artistic, a writer or a painter, and he wants peace and quiet and can't afford the city. New York's pretty expensive."

"You're right, it is. Go on, Mel. You're really doing well. I should turn this case over to you."

"Hardly. When would I work on it? From midnight to six A.M.?"

The plight of the working mother. We talked for a while, and then it was time for both of us to look after our children. Mel held Eddie and talked to him before she left, and he clearly loved it. I walked Mel and her kids to the front door and watched them skip down Pine Brook Road. Then I went back to Eddie and started our evening hour.

When he was happily asleep, I ate some leftovers from the weekend. When Jack came home later, I would sit with him while he ate. It amused me that there were now three family members, all of whom had different schedules. During the fifteen years I had been a nun at St. Stephen's, I had lived by the general schedule of the convent. We awoke at the same time, had morning prayers at the same time, performed our charges, taught our classes, came and went in the most efficient way possible. My life had now turned topsy-turvy.

I read a book as I ate, then took care of the dishes and grabbed the *Times*. The new family room was set up so that it was in a separate heating zone. I could keep Eddie warm upstairs and myself warm in the family room while leaving the kitchen, dining and living rooms cool. It even made sense now for Jack to have his late dinner in the family room so as not to have to heat the kitchen and the rest of the downstairs. I am a born penny-pincher, and doing things like this gives me, if not pleasure, at least satisfaction.

I sat back with the paper and started to read. The door was closed to save the heat and it took a moment before I realized the phone was ringing in the kitchen. I tossed the paper aside and dashed.

"Hello?"

"Chris? This is Jill Brady. We heard about Susan at work today."

"Yes. I found her body yesterday, upstate, about fifty miles from Brooklyn."

"The police came and interviewed us. I'll have to call them but I thought you'd like to hear first."

"Hear what?" I couldn't imagine what she had to tell me.

"I walked by my garage this evening on my way home. The car's been brought back."

"The car you lent to Susan?"

"Yes. I looked at the speedometer but I really can't remember how many miles were on it before, so I can't say how far it was driven. Are you sure she's dead?"

"As sure as I can be. Her face was beaten badly so we can't identify her that way, but the blood type's the same and so is the hair color. She was wearing jeans and a sweater from what I could see."

"Sounds like Susan. Well, I'll call that detective now and let him know. Maybe someone else drove the car back and they'll find fingerprints on the steering wheel. I didn't touch anything. I just opened the door and stuck my head in."

"Thank you for calling me first, Jill. This is a real shocker. It's possible the killer knew she had borrowed the car and where it was garaged."

"How would he know that?"

"She was very badly beaten. Maybe he got her to tell him things before he killed her."

"What a gruesome thought. By the way, I rang the bell of the people I rent the garage from. They didn't see anyone return the car, so for all we know, it's been there since last night."

"That's possible. We're not even sure when she was killed. There's no heat in the house and the body was frozen."

"This is a terrible conversation," Jill said. "I think I'll call the police now."

"Sounds like she went up to the farmhouse with her killer," Jack said when we talked about it later.

"It does, doesn't it?"

"Otherwise you've got the problem of an extra car if the killer drove his own."

"I hope he left some prints," I said.

"Don't count on it. He could have dumped the car somewhere it might not be found for weeks, but he didn't. This guy is smart. He knows enough about Susan that he knows she's borrowing a car, and when he comes back with it, he drops it off in the middle of the night so no one will see him. He's wearing gloves for warmth so there are no prints on the car and he walks to the nearest subway. Assuming he lives alone, he walks into his apartment like a guy coming home from a late date. Were the keys in the ignition?"

"I didn't ask."

"There's so damn much we don't know. When's your doctor's appointment?"

"Tomorrow before noon. I'm taking Eddie to Elsie's house after I nurse him."

"Kid's really getting around, New York for New Year's Eve, Elsie's tomorrow morning. Think any of this makes an impression on him?"

"I wish I knew."

10

The return of the car explained why there was none found at the farmhouse. If the killer had come in a separate car, there would have been one car too many at the murder scene. Now that was explained. Either he accompanied Susan from Brooklyn or she picked him up along the way—perhaps the person who had told her about the farmhouse five or six months ago?—and after he killed her he simply took her car and returned it to its parking place. As Jack had said, who would notice him in the middle of the night?

"So, Eddie," I said as I wrapped him in his tiny snowsuit on Tuesday morning, "we've solved a small mystery, but we have no answers for the big one."

His sleepy eyes looked at me for a moment, then closed. He had just finished nursing and was too sleepy to listen to my rambling. When I carried him out to the car, he never opened his eyes.

"Oh Chris, he's just so beautiful," Elsie Rivers said as she took my bundle out of my arms and nestled it in hers. "And look how much he's grown. What a blessing he is."

Elsie was my mother's closest friend and confidante during my childhood and was one of those remarkable women for whom each baby is a brand-new experience, no matter how many she has seen and fallen in love with.

For me, of course, Eddie was truly a first. I had almost nothing to do with babies for the first thirty-two years of my life, but Elsie had practically been born a grandmother, a woman who was drawn to babies the way I am to sweets. When she said how much he had grown, I had to smile. She could probably tell you to the ounce how much a baby would grow in a day, a week, or a month. For me it was a constant amazement at how he filled out his clothes a little more every few days without the benefit of steak and potatoes.

We spent only a few minutes talking since I had to get to my obstetrician on time, but I knew as I walked back to my car that Eddie was in the best of hands. With luck, I would return before he woke up but if he did, Elsie would charm him, I was sure.

This was my six-week checkup, the one that would give me a clean bill of health, a return to all the things I had become accustomed to in my life, including sex. I wondered, as I left the doctor's office, if I would ever feel wide-awake enough to engage in sex between feedings. But physically I was fine, and Dr. Campbell shook my hand and wished me a happy motherhood as I left. A nice woman, I thought as I put my coat on. A nice profession, too, treating women who were essentially healthy and doing something we all look forward to.

I took the opportunity to do some shopping before returning to Elsie's, where Eddie hadn't the least idea he'd been left with a sitter. She said he hadn't opened his eyes since I'd dropped him off!

Jack called in the afternoon to check up on my checkup. When I'd reported that all was well, he said, "I think there's an ID on Susan's body. I talked to the detective in charge and he said he was expecting the prints back momentarily."

"Has there been an autopsy yet?"

"I doubt it. That body's got to thaw before they can start. They're handling it locally. The Brooklyn detective should hear as soon as there's something. How's my son?"

"He's fine. Elsie was bitterly disappointed—he didn't even open his eyes."

"Kid takes after his old man."

"That's not so bad."

"Gotta go. See you later." There were background noises that indicated something was up.

It was Arnold who finally called with the news. "It's not Susan," he said.

"What?"

"They've checked the prints and they're not hers."

My mind was whirling. "Arnold, could Kevin have given the police prints he knew weren't Susan's?"

"He could have but he didn't. Ada gave the cops a few things that were Susan's, and some of those prints are the same as the prints from Kevin. Pretty compelling, and nothing matching the prints on the body."

"Who is she, then?"

"No one seems to know. She doesn't have an arrest record. A woman about Susan's age and build, similar hair color, wearing the same kind of clothes Susan wears—but doesn't everybody nowadays? Oh, and there were dental records. I forgot about those. Ada got some X rays from Susan's dentist and there's no comparison."

"This is wild."

"It's a lot worse than wild. The police are pretty sure Susan went up there. She seems to have been the one who rented the house last summer. And while they haven't said so, I get the feeling they think she could be the killer."

"That's terrible. We don't even know she was there. Are there any prints in the house that seem to be hers?"

"We'll find that out. Did you and Sister Joseph leave prints?"

"I don't know. Possibly. We had gloves on because it was so cold inside, but I went upstairs and looked through the only occupied bedroom—well, it had probably been occupied in warmer weather. It looked as though Susan—or the victim—had moved into the kitchen and was living there. Maybe I took my gloves off then. Is there a problem with having left prints?"

"No problem at all. The police know you were in the house."

"Arnold, Susan may not even have gone to that house on New Year's Eve."

"You and I know that. But she seems to have a connection to it; she rented it from the Donaldsons, she borrowed a car and said she was driving about fifty miles from Brooklyn, and she hasn't been seen since. All very circumstantial, not convincing to those of us with a brain, but you know how New York's Finest think." Arnold has never been known for flattering comments about police, Jack excluded.

"How on earth are they going to find out who that poor woman is? I didn't find a purse anywhere, or anything that looked like identification."

"They'll search their computers for reports of missing women. Eventually, they may have to use DNA, although they have prints from the body now and that may do the trick."

"This is just crazy. We have an unidentified body, a missing but presumably still alive Susan, no motive, and no connection."

"And an uncooperative boyfriend who probably knows more than he's letting on."

"Keep me posted, Arnold. I don't know what else to say."

"Nor I. How's the baby?"

"Doing fine. He smiles a lot."

"With a mother like you, how can he help it?"

That's why I love him.

Jack had heard the news by the time he came home from his classes but he'd been too busy to call.

"Puts everything in a new light, doesn't it?" he said.

"Puts everything in the dark as far as I'm concerned. Who is this woman? Who was the house rented by anyway, Susan or the victim? And why? Was it Susan's friend or the other woman's friend who suggested the farmhouse?"

"All good questions. Maybe Susan rented the house for herself and the victim came to visit her."

"And where's Susan?"

"You know, you have to consider she could be the killer."

"Oh, Jack."

"You going to eliminate a suspect because she's the daughter of a friend of your friend?"

"I have to figure out what's going on there—what went on there," I said, not answering his question. "Blackmail? How does a woman in her twenties get involved in blackmail? Something else?"

"There are certain relationships between women you may not want to think about," Jack said quietly.

I took a breath. "Hate the sin, love the sinner," I said. "But she had a boyfriend, Jack. She lived with a man."

"She lived with a man recently. What did she do two years ago? Three?"

Four, five, and six.

"You still want to keep on with this?"

"A woman has been murdered," I said firmly. "Nothing is worse than murder. I talked to Mel yesterday, and she came up with some good ideas for finding the person who led Susan to the farmhouse. I may look into that. Susan's friend Rachel might also be able to help."

"She might also have a handle on Susan's sexual preference."

"She might."

"And speaking of sexual preference, I have a very strong one for my wife."

I felt the cloud of fatigue lift. "That does something very nice to me."

"It was meant to. It's been a long time."

"Yes." I leaned over and kissed him, feeling the stirrings of lovely desires that had not been satisfied since late in my pregnancy.

"Think that guy upstairs is good till morning?"

"Count on it."

He put his arms around me and the rest, as they say, is sweet history.

11

I called Rachel Stone early Wednesday morning before she left for work. She didn't have time to talk, which didn't surprise me, but I had wanted to reach her early rather than wait for evening, and she called me back when she got to her job, a little after nine. Eddie was awake but quiet, so I was able to talk. Rachel had heard the terrible news that Susan was dead, but had not spoken to the Starks yesterday, and I was the one who was able to tell her that Susan was apparently alive and very much missing.

"God, what a relief," she said. "Does anyone know what happened?"

"About all we know for sure is that someone about Susan's age is dead in that farmhouse in Bladesville. They don't know who she is, but they're certain it isn't Susan because the fingerprints don't match. I want to ask you some questions, Rachel, some uncomfortable questions, and I hope you'll be truthful with me."

"I have nothing to hide," she said.

That, of course, wasn't the problem. "I'm going to come right out with it. Do you think Susan could have been having a relationship, a sexual relationship, with another woman?"

There was silence. Finally she said, "Susan?"

"Yes, Susan."

"I can't believe—Chris, what would make you ask such a thing?"

"I'm feeling my way. A woman has been murdered. Susan borrowed a car for a trip that was about fifty miles each way, just about the distance to that farmhouse. It looks as though Susan rented the house for herself or for the victim about five months ago. They knew each other. If we can figure out who the victim was, maybe it will lead us to Susan, and maybe it will also lead us to the murderer."

"Do you think Susan killed that woman?"

"I have no idea who killed her."

"Because I'm not going to say another word if that's where you're going. Susan is my friend. She's my best friend. I don't think she's capable of killing unless someone attacked her."

"That could have happened, you know."

"My head is buzzing. I've gone from being so relieved that Susan's not dead to having to consider her a killer, all in the space of a minute or two. Let me go back to your question. No, Susan is as heterosexual as they come. She's been going out since she was a teenager. With guys. She's in love with Kevin and I believe they have a good, healthy, physical relationship. Does that answer your questions?"

"Yes, it does." It meant that if there were anything sexual between Susan and another woman, Rachel didn't know about it. "Rachel, are you aware of Susan taking trips by herself in the last six months?"

"Without Kevin? Not unless she went away for a day and didn't tell me. But Kevin would know."

"I wonder," I said, thinking aloud, "whether she could have told Kevin she was staying overnight with her parents and then just gone upstate."

"I suppose—I suppose it could have happened. But

she would have been taking a big chance. If Kevin had to ask her something and she wasn't at the Starks', there would have been panic."

"That's exactly what happened on New Year's Eve."

"I see. Yes."

"So it's possible that she did it before and was just lucky not to be found out."

"Everything you say makes it seem as though something sinister was going on in Susan's life. I don't believe that's true. Secret maybe, but not sinister."

"We'll find out the truth eventually, Rachel. Thanks for being so forthright."

Eddie seemed quite content, so I took a chance and dialed *Single Up*, the magazine where Susan and Jill worked. Jill came on the phone and I told her the news.

"So it *was* Susan who returned the car," she said, with what sounded to me like relief.

"We don't know yet but I hope so. And if it was, she's in hiding somewhere."

"Well I would be, too, if I found a dead body, I can tell you."

"Jill, I want to ask you if Susan ever borrowed your car before last Thursday?"

"Never. I don't even think she knew I had one. She just happened to mention she was going to rent a car— no, that's not the way it was. I heard her on the phone talking to a rental agency and when she got off, I asked her if she'd like to borrow mine. She was hesitant, but I told her I'd really appreciate it, that sitting in a garage isn't the best thing for a car. So she said yes."

"Do you remember if Susan took time off from work in the last few months?"

"Oh boy." She exhaled. "You know, we run around a lot. There are days we have to go interview people or pick up photographs or get supplies. I really couldn't tell you. You know, Susan lives with someone. He's probably your best bet on something like that."

If he would tell what he knows, I thought. But we couldn't count on that. "Thanks for your help, Jill," I said.

"I hope you'll call me if she turns up."

I said I would. I hoped she would turn up.

I was afraid she wouldn't. There was a very dark possibility to all this, that someone, the person who was the link between Susan and the victim, had killed the woman in the farmhouse and taken Susan with him in Jill's car, hurting and eventually killing her. I had to find out what the connection was between the two women and who the "friend" was in the Bladesville area. I thought about Mel's suggestions as I nursed Eddie. Another retired teacher. Mrs. Halliday could help me with that. A commune. I would call Jack, and he could ask the local sheriff up there. They would surely know if such a thing existed. The idea of a commune sounded hopelessly out-of-date, one of those sixties' and seventies' phenomena. I imagined most of them were deserted now, the land lying fallow, the members having become part of the American mainstream, but who knew?

I put Eddie on my shoulder and patted his back, feeling his warm head next to my cheek. After the inevitable burp, I said, "There we go, little sweetheart," and began to nurse him on the second side.

A young family returning to the good earth. Someone she went to school with? Someone Rachel or Kevin might know? These were not easy things to check out. It occurred to me that I didn't know whose clothes those had been in the farmhouse, Susan's or the victim's. Which of them actually lived there? Joseph and I had been so sure the victim was Susan that we just assumed everything was hers. Now nothing seemed certain. I watched Eddie as he nursed. His eyes had been fixed on mine but now they were closing. He had been awake for a long time before eating and now the little eyelids were flickering, now closing. This was his soundest nap of the day, the time I had staked out as my own. Before he was fast asleep, I burped him again and put him in his crib. With a sigh, he nestled on the mattress. I leaned over and kissed him. Then I went downstairs to do my thing.

Jack called back pretty quickly. "If there's anything like a commune up there, the sheriff doesn't know about it and they would if there were, if you follow me. What made you think of something like that?"

"It was Mel's idea. She thought Susan might know someone on a commune who would know the farmhouse was empty. It was just a thought, Jack. It was the easiest to check out."

"Especially since I did the checking. Sorry, honey, it looks like you'll have to get another brainstorm."

"Aside from asking the neighbors, everything else is tougher. Mel said maybe another retired teacher lives up there. I can call Mrs. Halliday and ask her. Or maybe an artist or a writer that Susan knew from New York moved upstate to work in inexpensive peace and quiet."

"You'll just have to talk to Susan's friends and see if they can think of who that could be. This is really a weird one."

"Any word on whether Susan's prints were picked up in the house or the car?"

"Maybe later. I'll let you know. How's my boy?"

"Fed, changed, and fast asleep. This is when my brain gets working."

"Maybe a little snack would get mine working, too."

"That's a productive thought. Let me know if those prints match."

"You bet."

12

I could drive up there with Eddie and knock on doors along the road the farmhouse was on. Perhaps one of those families was the one Susan or the victim had known. And if not, perhaps they had met her in the last six months. Maybe there had been nights when she was cold or lonesome and craved the warmth of a fire or of neighbors. She might have spoken to them about who she was and why she was there. If I took Eddie with me, I could find a place to nurse him when he woke up hungry during the afternoon. It seemed a good idea.

I made myself a tuna fish salad sandwich, my old standby, and filled a thermos with skim milk. A few diapers, and I was ready. The car would be warm enough and Eddie would be in his snowsuit. If I had to, I could keep the motor and heater running while I nursed him.

I made a quick call to Brooklyn to tell Jack what I was going to do but he was out, so I gathered up my baby and his paraphernalia and went out to the car.

The day was nice but still very cold, colder up the Hudson than where we lived near Long Island Sound. It must have snowed a lot more up there, because the snow was still high and along the fields completely undisturbed, as white a blanket as I had ever seen. The glare was almost enough to require sunglasses but I had left them home.

I drove to the house nearest the Donaldson farm and pulled into the drive. Eddie was sleeping in his little seat and it seemed a good way to carry him. If they let me inside, I could put it on the floor, open his snowsuit, and not move him. He gave a few sighs as I lifted him out of the car, but that was all. The cold air didn't affect him. I walked up to the front door, thinking that a woman with a baby had to be the most disarming person in the world, and I rang the bell.

A small child opened the door and looked up at me. She had long blond hair and very blue eyes. She said, "Hi," and smiled shyly.

"Is your mommy home?" I asked.

"Uh-huh. Is that your baby?"

"Yes it is."

"She's pretty."

"It's a boy," I said.

"Oh."

"Could you call your mommy?"

"Uh-huh." She turned and ran, disappearing around a corner.

A minute later a young woman with exactly the coloring of the child appeared, holding a cloth that could have been a diaper or a dish towel. "Hi," she said, stopping before she reached me.

"Hi. I'm Chris Bennett. I wondered if I could talk to you for a few minutes."

"Are you selling something? Because if you are—"

"I'm not selling anything. I need some information."

"Come on in. I'm just feeding the baby."

"Thanks." I closed the door and followed her. "Can I leave mine here?"

"Sure. He's a little one, isn't he?"

"Six weeks old. My first. He should sleep soundly for a while and I'm not staying long." I pulled open the snaps on the snowsuit and eased Eddie's head out of the hood. A pull here and there and his little arms were out of the sleeves. Then I made my way to the kitchen where a small boy in a high chair was being fed and the little girl was helping herself to lunch at the table.

"I'm Dawn D'Agati," my hostess said, scooping up a spoonful of stuff in a jar and aiming it for the open mouth of the little boy. "What's this about?"

"About the incident next door," I said, not wanting to be too specific in front of the little girl.

"Uh, we better wait a while," Dawn said, glancing at her daughter. "Patti? How are you doing there, hon?"

"I'm done."

"You didn't finish your milk."

"I want a cookie to go with it."

"Drink your milk and then you can take a cookie upstairs. OK?"

Patti lifted the glass and drank with noisy gulps, her bright blue eyes looking at me above the rim. She was breathless when she put the glass down. "Can I have the cookie now?"

"Wait a minute." Dawn went to a box too high for her child to reach and pulled out a giant chocolate chip cookie. "Take it upstairs, OK?"

"OK."

I waited till Patti had scampered away before I explained what I was doing there.

"That whole thing is so creepy," Dawn said. "I'm scared to be alone here at night."

"It may not have been random violence," I said, hoping to ease her fears.

"God, I hope not. Fred wasn't supposed to rent out that house in the first place."

"I heard that."

"But he wanted the money, right?"

"I suppose so."

"So he rents it out to this girl and now she's dead."

I didn't correct her impression that the victim had rented the house. "Did you ever meet the girl that was living there?"

"Yeah, a couple of times. She came over one night and asked if we had any candles. There was no electricity there, you know that?"

"I gathered as much."

"And we talked. It was cold and she said the only room she had with heat was the kitchen. You know, the thermostat doesn't work without electricity, so it wasn't any use having a furnace."

"Do you remember her name?"

"Uh, uh—"

"Was it Susan?"

"Susan? No, it was something else."

I gave her a minute to remember while she wiped her son's face. "If you think of it—"

"It was like an abbreviation, D.D., I think. Yeah, that was it."

"You think it was the letters D-D, not DI-DI or DEE-DEE?"

"She said it was short for—I don't remember. Something fancy. But that's what it was."

"Did she tell you her last name?"

"If she did I don't remember."

"Have the police been by to ask you questions?"

"They came when I was out. My husband talked to them."

"Did this D.D. tell you what she was doing up here living in that old house?"

"She said she was working on a book."

"Did she tell you about the book?"

"No. She didn't seem to want to talk about it."

"Did she ever mention anyone named Susan?"

"She didn't talk about anybody that I can remember." She wiped the little boy's face again. "There you go, Snuggums. How 'bout a nap?"

He shook his head vigorously but reached his arms up to be lifted out of the high chair, and when Dawn had him in her arms, he laid his head on her shoulder and stuck his thumb in his mouth. I didn't think he'd last very long.

Dawn turned to face me and motioned that she was putting him to bed, as though saying it aloud would jinx the prospects.

I followed her out of the kitchen and went to look at my own little one. He was still fast asleep, and I waited quietly for Dawn to come downstairs.

"All quiet," she said with triumph, when she returned. "Let's sit in the kitchen. Looks like we've got a baby in every other room."

We sat at the kitchen table after Dawn cleared away her daughter's dishes and wiped down the high chair.

"Do you know what kind of car she drove?" I asked.

"I'm not sure she had one."

"How did she get here?"

"No idea. Someone must've dropped her off. I drove by there a lot and I never saw a car."

"Not even on New Year's Eve?"

She thought about it. "I don't think I drove by there on New Year's. Why? Should there have been a car?"

"Someone may have visited her."

"And killed her, right?"

"Maybe. Do you know how she happened to find Fred Donaldson? How she knew the house was empty?"

"She didn't say. It wasn't that kind of conversation.

She needed candles, and I told her to sit down while I looked for them. I had a coupla boxes of them—the electricity goes off here a lot in bad weather—so I gave her a whole box. Then we got to talking, and she told us about writing the book and then she said she hadda go. She wasn't here all that long."

"How did she get here?"

"She must've walked. Yeah, she walked. Because Jeff drove her home. My husband. He's real good that way."

"Isn't that a long walk?" I asked.

"Not so long. Down the other way it's, like, a mile till the next house but not here. It wouldn't take more than ten minutes."

"I wonder how she got her food," I said, "if she didn't have a car. It's a trip into town."

"Especially coming back," Dawn agreed. "It's uphill."

"So she must have known someone with a car," I suggested.

"I guess so. But she didn't say and I didn't ask."

"Did you get the impression that she lived here or that she came up from time to time?"

"I think she lived here, but don't hold me to it."

"What did she look like?"

"About your age. Lighter hair than yours, OK-looking but nothing special. She looked a little scruffy, if you know what I mean. Like a writer, right? Aren't they always living in an unheated attic somewhere?" She smiled.

"She hadn't made her first million yet," I said.

"I don't think she'd made her first dollar. She never paid us back for the candles. Not that I'm complaining," she added quickly. "I don't mean to speak ill of the dead. I'll tell you, we're thinking of putting an alarm system in the house now. You never know who's lurking around here at night, and sometimes Jeff doesn't come home till late."

"Why don't you wait a while, Dawn?" I said. "It might cost thousands, and the sheriff's department will probably find the killer pretty soon. A lot of murders are personal, you know, committed by someone who knew the victim."

"You think someone hated her?"

"I don't know. I don't even know who she was."

"Maybe she was writing one of those tell-all books and someone got mad."

"It could be." I took a piece of paper out of my notebook and wrote my name, address, and phone number on it. "If you think of anything, please give me a call. Was that the only time you ever saw her?"

"I waved to her sometimes when I drove by and she was outside. In the warm weather she would sit on the porch and read. And once I saw her in the store in town."

"Was she with anyone?"

"I couldn't tell you. Maybe. Oh, I see, you mean because she didn't have a car."

"I just wonder how she could have lugged a bunch of groceries back up here without a car."

"I don't know. Maybe the person who was with her was in another aisle."

"That's probably it," I said.

"And even after she saw me, she didn't remember the candles."

I drove back down the road away from the Donaldson farm to the next house with little hope that anyone there would have met either D.D. or Susan. Without a car there wasn't much chance either one of them would have hiked all this way to borrow something or have a chat. It didn't make much difference because no one was home.

I thought I would ask in the little restaurant in town and maybe the grocery store if I could find it. But first it was time for my tuna sandwich. I turned onto the main street of Bladesville about a quarter mile before the block that represented "downtown" and took out my lunch. Although my two and a half years of secular life had introduced me to finer culinary fare, I still found tuna fish salad to be especially satisfying in the way that foods from childhood often are. My mother had packed such sandwiches for my lunch, and Aunt Meg, with whom I lived for the next year, had followed suit, hoping to keep me not too unhappy after the loss of my mother.

By the time I had downed the skim milk and put my trash back in the bag, Eddie was making little whimpers I could not ignore. "I bet you're getting hungry," I said, taking him on my lap and beginning to change him. It wasn't easy but when he was in a dry diaper, I opened my clothes and began to nurse him. He seemed utterly oblivous to where we were, his interest being in filling his stomach. When he finished at the first breast, I put him on my shoulder and burped him, then rearranged myself so he could nurse on the other side.

He had hardly started when I heard a loud rap on the window. Startled and a little confused, I pulled my coat over Eddie and my somewhat bare breast, and turned to look at the intruder. It was a man in a tan uniform.

I wound the window down slightly. "Yes?" I said, thinking I must have parked illegally, although I was off the road and there were no signs.

"You can't do that here," he said, looking angry.

"I'm sorry?"

"You can't nurse that baby here. You have to go indoors. It's not allowed."

"I can't go indoors, Officer. I live fifty miles from here."

"Well, you should've thought of that before you drove to Bladesville. You better stop that right now or you're going to have to come with me."

I am not a confrontational person. In fact, I usually try to avoid confrontations, whatever the cost. But suddenly I was angry. "Have I violated a law?" I asked as calmly as I could.

"You're exposing yourself in public. There are laws against that."

"I'm sure nursing mothers aren't included in laws on public exposure," I said.

"Ma'am, I've asked you to stop. I want you to stop what you're doing and cover yourself up."

"I'll cover myself up when my baby has finished nursing." I said it with a false calm but I could feel the beginnings of panic.

"I'm gonna have to take you in." He said this with resignation, as though he knew he had pushed this too far.

"Do you intend to handcuff me?" I asked with more starch in my voice than I had intended.

"No ma'am, I do not. I would like some identification from you right now."

I braced Eddie with one arm and leaned over him to reach my handbag. With difficulty I pulled out my wallet and gave the officer my driver's license.

He looked at it and copied down information. Then he went back to his car and I saw in the rearview mirror that he was talking on the radio. It occurred to me that he was checking to see if I was driving a stolen car or was wanted for some crime even greater than nursing my baby in public.

He returned a minute later. "OK, I want you to follow me to the station house, Mrs. Brooks. Don't try anything foolish because I've got your license right here."

"You have no right to that license," I said, becoming angrier. "I was not involved in an automobile incident."

"Sorry, ma'am, you gave it to me voluntarily and I'm holding onto it till we settle this at the station."

"I'll follow you," I said, "as soon as my baby finishes nursing. Are you afraid I'll flee the scene of the crime?" I knew I was overdoing it but I was really angry. This was a young man, possibly no older than I was, and he was enforcing a code of morality that had probably never been very popular and certainly had never been universal, a code I disagreed with more strongly than I had ever realized.

He went back to his car and pulled up in front of mine. Eddie slowly finished, falling briefly asleep. I put him on my shoulder, aware that the cop was watching in his mirror, and patted his back. Then I took my time and changed him, imagining the officer seething as he waited. When Eddie was in his seat in the back of the car and I was completely dressed again, I started the motor. The idiot in the car ahead actually turned on his flashing lights as he led the way to my moment of truth.

13

The sergeant sitting behind a raised counter in the small station house in the next town looked like an old bulldog. His head was large, his hair dark and slightly graying, and his big face was lined with a permanent look of droopy sadness. The look intensified when he heard the deputy's complaint and glanced over at me and the baby on my shoulder.

"You sure about this, Kovacs?" he said.

"Yes sir," Deputy Kovacs said, and quoted the number of an ordinance that I had presumably violated.

"Can I see some identification, ma'am?" the sergeant asked, after apparently thinking things over.

I turned to Deputy Kovacs. "I think you have my driver's license," I said.

He pulled it out of his pocket and handed it to the sergeant. The sergeant looked at it, pulled out a form, and wrote on it. Then he looked down at me. "Here's what we're going to do," he said. "I'm going to let you go on your own recognizance. You'll be notified of the date for the hearing and the location, and you're required by the laws of New York to show up on that day."

"May I call my lawyer now?"

"Call anyone you like. Phone's over there." He pointed to a pair of pay phones on the wall.

I pulled out a bunch of quarters as I sat on the hard

bench, wondering what on earth was wrong with me. Jack had suggested at least twenty times that I get a telephone credit card *in case of emergency* and I had refused every time because of my stupid principles. What principle could possibly be involved in being able to make a phone call from a pay phone? Holding a bunch of quarters in my hand and my baby over my left shoulder, I dialed Arnold's number from memory. He was there and they put him on, my panic subsiding as I heard his voice.

"What's up?"

"I've been arrested, Arnold." I wasn't sure if that was true or not.

"Where? What for?"

"I'm in the town next to Bladesville. Silverton, I think it's called. I was nursing Eddie in the car, and a deputy came along and said I was exposing myself."

He made a sound I could not interpret. "You want to get very rich, Chrissie? We'll sue hell out of them. You nursed your baby in one of the three states in this splendid union of ours that expressly permits the nursing of babies in public."

"Are you sure?" I knew it was a dumb question, but I couldn't believe I could be so lucky.

"Haven't lost all my marbles yet. Let me talk to whoever's in charge there."

I turned to the sergeant. "Could you talk to my attorney, sergeant?"

He growled slightly and raised himself from his chair, descended from the platform, and picked up the phone. "Sergeant Terence Farley here, town of Silverton. Who am I speaking to?"

It wasn't a long conversation. Deputy Kovacs watched and listened calmly as I sat, my spirits rising. They would have a fine surprise, these two less than well-informed law enforcers.

The sergeant put down the phone, opened a door, and disappeared. It was several minutes before he came back. "Kovacs?" he said, his bulldog face looking very grim.

They had a short, quiet talk and then the sergeant turned to me. "You're free to go, Mrs. Brooks. I apologize for the error." He went to his desk and tore up the form he had filled out.

Deputy Kovacs left without saying a word. I decided Eddie and I had outstayed our welcome and I followed him.

"He tried to make me feel like a flasher," I said to Arnold on the phone when we got home. "He used the phrase 'exposing yourself in public' as if I'd stood in the town square and taken my clothes off."

"Well, you ought to get a written apology from them. If you don't, I'll hound them a little. You find out anything, or did they pick you up before you could? I don't suppose you went up there to push your baby carriage in the snow."

I told him about my conversation with Dawn D'Agati.

"So we have a first name for the deceased. Never heard it from the cops up there. They must be all tied up arresting nursing mothers."

"Dawn said the police came by and talked to her husband. He probably didn't remember the woman's name. They didn't come back to talk to her. She thought the name D.D. was an abbreviation for a first and middle name but she can't remember them. What I need to do is figure out how to find the person who told Susan the farmhouse was empty. It wasn't the D'Agatis. And it didn't sound as though D.D. knew many people up there."

"Well, keep thinking. Something'll come to you."

When I hung up, it did.

* * *

It was too late to do much about it, but I was able to reach Jack. I kept the news of my arrest for later when he came home. "Maybe Susan knew a real estate agent," I said.

"Good thinking. I'll check the phone book and get you a list—if there's more than one up there."

"Great. I think I'll make another trip up there tomorrow."

"I'll bring the list home. Kiss my boy for me."

"I will."

Real estate agents. That might be the wrong way to go but it was certainly a good place to start. Any realtor in the area would have known when the Donaldson farm was put up for sale and later that a large piece of it had been sold, leaving an empty house on a smaller piece of land. But it was more likely a person who knew the property personally who would tell a city girl off the record that the house was empty, and with luck she might make a deal for it.

Jack came home after ten and went upstairs to change and look in on his son while I heated up his dinner. When he came back and sat down to eat, I sprang my surprise on him.

"You were what?" he half shouted.

"Well, sort of arrested. I was taken to the station house, the one Joseph and I went to. You have a lewd wife, dear husband, in case you never noticed."

"I sure as hell never noticed. I can't believe this. We've got a law in New York State that says—"

"I know. Arnold informed me and told the sergeant, and then they let me go. Arnold asked me if I wanted to sue them for a million dollars."

"And?"

"And you know what I said. But they really do owe me an apology, and not just because what I did was legal. There was nothing morally wrong with it. They embarrassed me, they frightened me—I really felt panic creeping up when I was sitting in that station house—and the whole thing was absurd. I was fantasizing about taking the case to the Supreme Court and having all the nuns of St. Stephen's sitting in on the trial to support me."

"You think they'd all support you?"

"I'm not sure, but it was a great image."

"Why didn't you call me, Chris?"

"Because I didn't want to win it with one cop talking to another cop. This was an issue for me; it was something I believed in. I was willing to fight for it."

"Wow. You're looking more and more like that tough nun of my childhood who—"

"Sister Merciless?"

He actually reddened a little. "One and the same."

"I'm not. I just came to a point in my life when I knew I had to stand up for a principle. Do you suppose it's motherhood that's done this to me?"

"Ah, probably it's listening to me talk about the cases in my classes. Although motherhood's been known to have pretty strong effects on women."

"Well, I'm glad it ended quickly and I got home in time to get Eddie ready for bed, but I hope that Deputy Kovacs thinks twice before he considers nursing to be lewd."

"I got a hunch he will. Here's the list of realtors in the Bladesville area."

I looked it over. "I'll call and find out who the listing realtor is before I go, and start there."

"Taking Eddie?"

"Not this time. Elsie said she'd be delighted to have

him, and if he doesn't wake up of his own accord, she'll stick pins in him."

"Sounds like the beginning of a great relationship."

At nine on Thursday morning I called the real estate agency on Jack's list that seemed to be closest to Bladesville. (It occurred to me that if I'd had my wits about me I could have looked at the FOR SALE sign in front of the farmhouse and found out the easy way.) They weren't the listing realtors, and the woman I talked to wasn't anxious to give me their name. "I can help you with that property if you're interested." But finally she gave me the name, Town and Country Properties, which seemed appropriate for the area, and said she would love to help me.

I then called Town and Country and asked for the agent who listed the Donaldson farm.

"This is George Gleason," a deep voice said.

"Mr. Gleason, my name is Chris Bennett and I'm going to be in your area today. Will you be in between noon and one?"

"Absolutely, Ms. Bennett. I understand you're interested in the Donaldson farmhouse."

"I have some questions to ask you about it, yes."

"Well, I'll wait for you."

He gave me directions and I was set.

Naturally, as soon as I heard the words Town and Country I remembered them from the sign at the house. I thought it was interesting that George Gleason didn't mention that he couldn't take me inside the property—it was still a crime scene, as far as I knew—but since I wasn't really interested in buying, a conversation would be enough for me.

I found the real estate office with no difficulty. It was a

storefront between a small bank and a laundromat on a street that looked very much like the main street of Bladesville. When I walked inside, a large man rose from a desk and greeted me with a smile.

"Ms. Bennett?"

"Yes. Thank you for waiting." I sat down in the customer's chair next to his desk, my back to the front of the office. "Mr. Gleason, I'm not here as a prospective buyer. I need some information, in absolute confidence, and I'm hoping you can give it to me."

"You've got my ear," he said genially. "Can't imagine what I know that would be of interest."

"I know a murder was committed in that house last week."

His face fell. "This was a very, very sad situation. No one even knew that woman was living there. She must have been some kind of squatter."

"She wasn't," I said. "She was renting the house from Mr. Donaldson. I have no intention of getting anyone in trouble over this. I'm trying to find out who the woman was."

"I see." He closed his eyes and nodded his head. "Now I understand."

"Understand what?"

"Fred Donaldson called me last summer and said he wanted the key to the house back. That if anyone wanted to see the house, he had to be told first."

"So he could warn her to pack up and get out."

"That's the way it looks, doesn't it? I had no part in this."

Somehow I believed him. He had seemed genuinely surprised to learn that the murdered woman wasn't a squatter. "Mr. Donaldson told me that a woman came to him and asked to rent the house. That woman was not the victim but another woman who's now missing. She told him that someone who lived around here told her the house was empty and who it belonged to."

"Someone else rented that house?"

I took Susan's picture out of my bag and showed it to him. "He and his wife identified her as the renter."

He studied it, then shook his head. "Never saw her in my life."

I heard the front door open and a woman called, "Hi, George."

He waved to the voice behind me. "Go on," he said. "This is very interesting."

"I really need to find the person she knew who told her about the farmhouse. I think it may well have been someone in this office."

"I think I'll catch some lunch, George," a man's voice called from behind where I was sitting.

"See you later, Larry."

I turned and caught a glimpse of the man who was leaving. "I guess I'm keeping you from your lunch," I said.

"Not to worry. In this business, you grab it when you can. Now let me assure you that everyone in this office is a licensed broker and wouldn't do what you suggested. They could lose their licenses. That house was condemned and Fred may get himself into a bunch of trouble for renting it. Not to mention what'll happen when the IRS gets hold of this."

"I'm a friend of the family of the young woman in the picture. I have no interest in getting anyone in trouble. Susan is missing and everyone is very upset about it. We don't know if she's alive or dead. But she knew someone up here, and no one in her family or among her friends has any idea who that person is. I'm not turning anyone in to the authorities or the IRS. I just want to find the person who told her about the farmhouse."

"You got me," George Gleason said. "I don't know this woman. I don't know anything about it." He handed me the picture.

"May I talk to the people in the office?"

"Be my guest. Alice Konig is at her desk. Larry Dickens just went to lunch. There are a couple of others, but they're not here now. You looking for a man or woman?"

"I wish I knew."

He took a piece of paper and wrote names and addresses. I thanked him and went to Alice Konig's desk and talked to her for a few minutes. She said she knew nothing and although she smiled a lot, I thought she was very uncomfortable with my questions. But being uncomfortable didn't mean she was the person.

While we were talking, George Gleason said he was going to lunch. A few minutes later I decided it was time for me to have mine. There was a sandwich in the car and I was hungry. I said good-bye to Mrs. Konig and left the office.

My car was a few doors down the street. I stopped and fished for my keys outside the realtor's, then walked down the block.

"Excuse me."

I turned around. A man stood next to me. He was mid-thirties, dark hair, vaguely familiar. "Yes?"

"You never saw me and I never gave this to you." He handed me a small square of pink paper with writing on it. "I don't understand," I said, feeling confused.

"That's all I'm saying." He turned and walked up the street to the Town and Country Properties office and went inside.

I looked at the note. It said *Teddy Toledo*, and had an address and a phone number. The address was in a town I had driven through to get to Silverton and Bladesville.

I started back to the real estate office and then stopped. The man who had given me the note was the Larry who had gone to lunch while I was talking to George Gleason. He must have heard our conversation. This Teddy Toledo had to be the link I was looking for.

14

I sat in my car eating my sandwich and drinking skim milk from my thermos, hoping there was nothing lewd about my actions. According to the piece of paper on the seat beside me, Teddy Toledo lived in Stormkill. I recognized the "kill" part of the name as a Dutch word that many old towns, like Peekskill, had, a relic of the early settlers of the Hudson River valley.

The question was, should I knock on Teddy Toledo's door by myself? I really had no desire to go to the Bladesville sheriff and tell him I had a possible lead in the murder of D.D. Doe. But I didn't know if Teddy Toledo was a dangerous person.

Just to be on the safe side, I found a pay phone and left a message for Jack, who was away from his desk, that I was going to Toledo's house. A nearby gas station gave me directions to the road in Stormkill where Toledo lived.

It was a big, old house with an apartment over the garage, and I wondered whether Mr. Toledo might be the tenant up there. I started by ringing the doorbell at the main house, and a gray-haired woman answered. She had a bright smile and wore wool pants and a sweater.

"Oh, you're looking for Teddy," she said, when I explained my mission. "He lives up there." She stepped out of the house and pointed to the garage.

"Do you know if he's home?"

"Oh, I think so. His car's there. I don't think he takes his walk till later on. Just go up the stairs and knock on his door."

I felt better about visiting this man if someone nearby knew I was there. The stairs to the apartment door were brushed clean of snow, as had been the walkway from the house. I wondered if that was part of his job as tenant. There was a small landing at the top of the stairs, and I held my breath a minute before knocking.

"Coming," came the brisk reply and the door was whipped open. "Oh. Sorry. I was expecting Mrs. Anderson."

"She told me to knock on your door. Mr. Toledo?"

"Yeah."

"I'm Chris Bennett. I'd like to—"

"Come inside. It's freezing out there."

"Thank you."

The apartment was one large room with a tiny kitchen to the right of the door, a wall of closets, and an open door to a small bathroom, an efficient use of the space of a two-car garage. But only a small part of that space was used for living. Teddy Toledo, a thirtyish man in jeans and a sweatshirt with a blond beard and a bit of a stomach, was indeed an artist, one of Melanie's suggestions. Easels and drop cloths and canvases and paints took up about three-quarters of the large room.

"You're an artist," I said.

"If you're from the IRS, I'm aspiring. If you're here to buy, yes, I'm an artist, and everything's for sale."

"I'm neither," I said, but I rather liked him. "I want to ask you about Susan Stark."

"Who?" He pulled a chair away from a small kitchen table and offered it to me.

"Susan Stark."

"Never heard of her. She a fan of my work?"

"I thought she was a friend." I took my coat off and he took it from me, hanging it in one of the most crowded closets I had ever seen. "I thought you were the one who told her about the Donaldson farmhouse."

"Who are you?"

"Susan is missing," I said. "I'm looking for her. Her parents are frantic, her boyfriend is beside himself. I just want to know where she is." I had been going to say "if she's dead or alive" but I thought better of it.

"I've never heard the name, and I don't know what farmhouse you're talking about."

I took the picture of Susan out of my bag and handed it to him. He looked at it quite intently and I half expected him to comment on her bone structure, but he handed it back. "Sorry."

"Mr. Toledo, Susan rented that farmhouse in Bladesville five months ago from Fred Donaldson. She said you had told her it was vacant." It was a lie and I hate to lie, but I couldn't mention the realtor who had given me Toledo's name and address.

"She gave him my name?"

"Yes."

"And she said her name was Susan Something?"

"I'm not sure what name she gave him."

"I don't know what you're talking about, OK? And I don't have a lot of time to kill. So if you don't mind—"

And then it hit me: Fred Donaldson's uncertainty that the picture of Susan was the same person who had rented the house. "Did D.D. rent the farmhouse?"

"Yeah, D.D. rented it," he said, after a pause during which he must have decided to tell me the truth. "Let me see that picture again."

I gave it to him.

"There's a resemblance, but this isn't D.D. The hair color's the same, something about the face is similar."

"Mrs. Donaldson thought this was the person they rented the house to."

"Maybe if you saw D.D. once and then you saw this picture a couple of months later, you could make that mistake."

"Do you know what happened to D.D.?"

"What do you mean? Is she gone? I haven't seen her since last week."

How do you know when a person is telling the truth? I had just told a little white lie and there was a good chance Toledo had not recognized it as such. If he didn't know D.D. was dead, he probably had had nothing to do with Susan's disappearance. But if he were D.D.'s killer . . . "She's dead," I said. "I'm sorry to be the one to tell you."

He looked at me with a face full of shock. "What happened to her?"

"She appears to have been murdered."

"Someone killed D.D.?"

"That's right."

He lifted his shoulders and turned his hands out. "Why?" he asked as though it were the last thing in the world he could imagine happening.

"I was hoping you could help me find that out."

"Look, I'm not saying another thing till you tell me who you are and what your interest is in all this."

"My name is Christine Bennett," I said. "I know Susan Stark's parents."

"Who the hell is Susan Stark?" he shouted.

"She's a young woman who disappeared the day before New Year's Eve. I have reason to believe that she went to the farmhouse owned by Fred Donaldson. I thought until a moment ago that she had rented that house, although I can't tell you why she would do that. I can't even tell you what her connection is to D.D. But she borrowed a car last Thursday in Brooklyn and told the owner she was going to make approximately a hundred-mile round-trip, which would be just about to Bladesville and back. She seems to have known about the Donaldson farmhouse, although if she didn't rent the house, I don't know how or why. I'm not making a lot of sense, am I?"

"Very little. If there's a Susan Stark in D.D.'s life, she didn't tell me about her."

"May I ask how you know D.D.?"

"We met in New York, a year and a half, maybe two years ago. We were friends. I wanted to get out of the city and I heard about this place, talked to Mrs. Anderson, and I got it. I've been here over a year. I kept in touch with D.D. and when she said she'd like to quit the city herself, I let her know about the farmhouse."

I noticed he didn't mention anything about how he had found his apartment or heard about the Donaldson farmhouse, and I assumed he had made both finds through his friend at the real estate office.

"Did D.D. have a car?" I asked.

"Nah. You can't have a car in New York. You spend your whole life moving it from one side of the street to the other." He was referring to the alternate-side parking restrictions because of street cleaning.

"Then you drove her up here?"

"I think she rented a station wagon when she came up."

"How did she get out to buy groceries? She was pretty far from the center of town."

"I'd pick her up, usually. We got together every once in a while. I was going to drop over tomorrow."

"Did she have a phone?"

"She could hardly afford to keep herself fed. She

didn't have a phone. She didn't even have electricity. My God, I can't believe she's dead."

"Mr. Toledo—"

"Call me Teddy, OK?"

"Teddy, what is D.D.'s full name?"

"Let's see. It's Delilah D. Butler. Her mother had great aspirations for her. Donna, I think, is her middle name. D.D. couldn't stand the Delilah. I think it hurt her every time she had to write it."

"Do you have an address for her? Before she moved up here?"

"Yeah, but she's been gone since the summer. Wait a minute. I'll get the street number for you." He went to the closet and pulled something off a shelf. "Here. It's over on the Lower East Side, not the kind of place you could stay in for long. Lots of animal life."

I copied it down. The Lower East Side is one of the oldest parts of Manhattan, the first to be settled. When civilization moved north, which is uptown, the old buildings were left to age and crumble.

"What did she work at?"

"Whatever pleased her at the moment is the impression I got. She took some great pictures of celebrities and sold them for enough money to live on for a while."

"Then she didn't have what you'd call a regular job."

"I didn't know her that long. In the time I knew her, she did a few things, and that was one of them. For a couple of months she was a messenger and rode a bike through New York, delivering stuff. Then she turned around and wrote an article about it for one of the magazines. She was a talented person but—"

"But what?"

"Something was bothering her."

That's what Kevin had said about Susan. "You have any idea what?"

"Not really. We were friends, not lovers. She talked to me about a lot of things, but she held some back. It was just something I could tell, a strong feeling. You want a beer?"

"No thanks."

He went to a small refrigerator and took out a bottle, opened it, and drank from the bottle. "There's a micro-brewery up here. I'm their best customer."

"How old was she?" I asked.

"I'd guess thirty, give or take."

"Was she working on some project up here?"

"She was planning something."

"What does that mean?"

"It means that's what she told me, and that's all she told me. She may also have been writing some stuff, but I'm not sure. In the summer she kept one of the upstairs rooms as a study and she had an old manual typewriter there that she used. But when it got cold, she had to move into the kitchen where there was a woodstove. It was the only room that had any heat. I think she may have put the typewriter in there, too, but I'm not sure. I've been there, but the room was so full of junk I couldn't tell you what she had."

"She was planning something," I said.

"That's what she told me."

"What was your impression? Was it something that would make money? Was it an act of revenge? Would it make her famous?"

"I don't think D.D. gave a damn about money. She knew how to make enough to survive. If she had a taste for good clothes and expensive jewelry, it didn't show. So I don't think it was that. Maybe she had a thing for fame. She had a good time photographing those celebs. Maybe she decided to be one of them, but I couldn't tell you how she'd manage it."

"And revenge? Was she angry at anyone? Did one of those people she worked for do something to hurt her? Or a man she knew?"

"You're asking me to speculate," Teddy said, putting the bottle of beer on the table. "This is a person I didn't know very well until she came up here last summer. I liked her. We ate together sometimes in the city, and out here, too. But I never met a friend of hers, never heard her mention a sister or brother. You know what? I think she sold those pictures to *Cool* magazine."

"That's something," I said gratefully.

"Or maybe it was the article. I really don't remember."

"You have a phone here?"

"Sure." He pointed.

I walked over and copied down the number. Then I wrote my own down for him. "Did D.D. mention New Year's Eve to you as a time when this thing she was planning would come to fruition?"

He thought about it. "I don't think she ever said that, but she did tell me not to drop by over New Year's."

"Was she expecting company?"

"She didn't say. But when I dropped her off last week—Wednesday, I think it was—she said not to drop in over the weekend. I do that sometimes, but I've been pretty busy myself or I'd've gone to see her already. It's over a week."

Wednesday was the day Kevin had presumably dropped Susan off at the Starks'. Thursday was the day she had told Jill Brady she was going to use the car. Had D.D. Butler been expecting her?

I handed Teddy the paper with my name and phone number.

He looked at it. "Wait a minute," he said. "I'm really not thinking clearly. D.D. carried a purse as big as a steamer trunk. There must be ID in there and phone numbers for everyone she knew. Why are you asking me?"

"There was no purse, no ID, nothing at all in the house."

"You mean the killer took it all?"

"It looks that way."

"Why would anyone do that?"

"The sheriff thinks that since winter isn't the time for prospective buyers to look at farms, the body might not have been discovered for many months and by that time it might not be identifiable."

"But I dropped by every week."

"Then the killer didn't know that." Unless Teddy was the killer. And after murdering D.D. and disposing of her effects, he just decided not to drop by. Ever again.

15

"So this Teddy Toledo set her up in the Donaldson farmhouse and drove her into town from time to time so she didn't starve to death." Jack was eating his late dinner and I had finished my tale.

"And unless she gave her name to the local shop-keepers in Bladesville, he may have been the only person for fifty miles, with the exception of the D'Agatis, who knew who she was and where she was living."

"Nice. And then you breeze in this afternoon and it looks like you're the second person in fifty miles who knows about D.D. And she's dead."

"You sound as though you think he's a suspect."

"Damn right he's a suspect. He's got this girl in a farmhouse where she can't even tell people she's living because it's illegal for her to be there. There's no mail delivery. She pays no utility bills. She has no car so he's her sole transportation. She can't call for help because she has no phone. You think he's *not* a suspect?"

"He seems like a pretty mild guy," I said meekly. After all, I'd been alone with him for half an hour or so, and I didn't like to think he'd done to D.D. Butler what someone had done to her.

"It's the neatest setup I've ever seen," Jack said with enthusiasm. "Nobody except you can even connect him with the house. You said Fred Donaldson told you she gave an obviously phony name when she rented the house."

"She did."

"It was a stroke of luck that the guy in the real estate office even put you on to Toledo. If the sheriff's deputies had come around, which they wouldn't have much reason to do, he might have said nothing."

I agreed with that. "Anyway, I've got an address here for some rat-infested place that D.D. Butler lived in before she moved up to Bladesville. I doubt whether the Welcome Wagon lady comes around, and I don't know if it's the kind of place where you know your neighbors."

"And I don't know if it's the kind of place you want to visit unarmed," Jack said, looking at the address. "No," he said quickly. "I'm not entirely serious. But that's not an upscale neighborhood."

"That was the impression I got from Teddy."

"Oh, it's Teddy. No wonder you don't suspect him."

I smiled. "You're right that he had the perfect opportunity, especially if he kept her whereabouts secret and she never went farther than the D'Agati house down the road. But there's no motive, Jack. And he said she was planning something."

"Planning what?"

"He didn't know and she didn't tell him. Call it intuition. And she told him not to drop by over the New Year's weekend."

"Ah."

When I hear that syllable, I know I've struck a chord. "Right. The last time he saw her, or admits to having seen her, was the Wednesday before New Year's. That's the day Susan was dropped off—"

"Allegedly."

"Allegedly, by Kevin at the Starks' house. And that night or the next day she borrowed Jill Brady's car to make a hundred-mile trip. It almost sounds as if D.D. was expecting Susan."

"And we don't know what for."

"We also don't know if it ever happened. But whatever it's worth, we now know that Susan didn't rent the farmhouse; D.D. did."

"So it's possible," Jack said, taking a piece of paper and folding it in quarters in his usual way, "that Susan and D.D. never met or at least never met before New Year's Eve."

"Definitely possible."

"Which would mean that Susan found out where D.D. was living in much the same way you found out about the farmhouse, asking a bunch of people a bunch of questions."

"Except she was looking for D.D. and I was looking for Susan."

"So why was she looking for D.D.?"

"That is the question."

"You're sounding poetic. Looking forward to going back to work?"

My work was teaching poetry so his comment wasn't far-fetched. "I think so. Elsie will probably pay me to leave Eddie with her. It sounds like they entertained each other all afternoon."

"Couldn't be better. By the way, have you given all this info to Arnold?"

"I called when I got home but he wasn't there. I'll talk to him tomorrow."

"Well, you talk to him. I'm going to call the Starks' resident precinct and tell them what you learned. It should make the detective who caught the case very happy, lots more info for the file with no effort on his part."

"Fine. Let them deal with the Bladesville and Silverton police department. I never want to go back to that station house in my life."

"Understood. And you sure don't want to hurt their tender feelings by showing off how much you've learned while they were arresting nursing mothers."

"Exactly."

"Well, you're way ahead of them, honey. Not that I'm surprised. Just watch your step, OK? Spending an afternoon with a possible killer can pose a challenge to your security, if you get my meaning. And Eddie's future."

"It's all I think about."

Nothing was truer.

Friday morning I called Arnold, but he wasn't in his office. I took out the Manhattan telephone book and looked up *Cool* magazine. There wasn't any. I felt a little chill. Maybe Teddy had lied to me to put me off. I could call him and check the name, but I had the feeling he might be a night person and would not appreciate my waking him. I put the phone book on my lap and ran my finger down the list of entries starting with Cool. There was Cool Air, Cool Cars, Cool Clothes, Cool Harry J., Inc., Cool Sound, and *Cool Times*. I decided to call the last listing.

A bright young voice answered, "Good morning, *Cool Times*."

"Is this the magazine?" I asked.

"Yes, it is. How can I help you?"

"I'm trying to locate someone who had something published in your magazine recently."

"One moment. I'll connect you."

The next voice said, "Billy Luft."

"Mr. Luft, my name is Christine Bennett. I'm trying to locate D.D. Butler. She had something published in your magazine recently."

"D.D., yeah, some pictures, a photo-essay. Nice spread. We got a lot of good comments on that."

"Do you have an address for her?"

"Got her old one." He read it off to me, the same address Teddy Toledo had given me. "I don't think she lives there any more. She said she was moving and she didn't leave a forwarding address."

"Does she have an agent or a manager?" I asked hopefully.

"Works on her own. I met her, which is how we got together. If you talk to her, tell her I'd like more from her."

I decided not to tell him what had happened. "Do you know any of her friends? I'd really like to find her."

"I saw her once with a guy named Harlow Sugar."

"Sugar?"

"Like in coffee. I don't have a number for him but there can't be too many in the book."

"Thank you, Mr. Luft."

"No thanks necessary. I haven't been called 'Mr.' since I was twelve years old."

I had hardly hung up when Jack called. "Susan's prints are in Jill Brady's car. Not a lot of them. She was probably wearing gloves most of the time."

"Anybody else's?"

"Probably Jill's. She balked at being printed. Anyway, none of the other prints belong to anyone on file."

"So no known criminal drove the car recently."

"Not with his gloves off."

"Doesn't tell us much. Uh-oh, I hear someone crying."

"Go do your thing."

I was nursing Eddie when the phone rang. I gathered him up and grabbed a chair on my way to answer it.

"Chris? It's Arnold."

"Arnold, I've been trying to reach you since yesterday. I've got a bunch of stuff to tell you."

"Before you start, I have something to tell you." He sounded very somber and I flinched, expecting the worst. "This isn't easy. Something has come up in the Susan Stark case, and I have to ask you to stop looking into it."

"I don't understand. Have they found her body?"

"Susan came home yesterday. She's alive and well and we're all relieved to see her."

"Then—"

"I'm afraid she's the number-one suspect in the killing of the woman in Bladesville."

"Has she been charged?"

"It's a matter of time. Her prints were found in the farmhouse so they can tie her to the location. I'm representing her, and I have to ask you to stop your investigation and go no further."

"Arnold, I don't know what to say."

"We'll talk about it when it's over. Susan didn't kill that woman or anyone else, but the hick cops have no suspects. They still don't even know who she is."

"I know," I said.

"You may think you do but it's a lot more complicated than what it appears to be."

"I don't know what to say," I said again.

"The best thing is to forget about this. I know you've been as worried as the rest of us about Susan. But she's safe and sound now, and I have a lot of work ahead of me to see to it that she isn't wrongly convicted of a terrible crime."

"I understand," I said, feeling as low as I had ever felt.

"We'll talk again, Chrissie. There's nothing personal in this, you understand that."

"Arnold, suppose I can prove she's innocent?"

"I don't want you involved in the case in any way," he said.

"OK."

Eddie finished nursing and I eased him up to my shoulder. I needed two hands. I said good-bye.

I sat in my rocker with Eddie on my shoulder for a long time after I changed him. Arnold thought Susan was guilty. Why else would he refuse my offer to try to clear her? He was afraid that the more information I turned up, the more guilty she would appear. By now she would have told Arnold what her connection to D.D. Butler was, what there was between them that had precipitated their meeting. I was still totally in the dark about all that.

But I had to admit that I felt hurt. I had been summarily dismissed from a case that was not only interesting, but urgent and vital. And even though Susan had reappeared, the case itself, though somewhat changed, was no less interesting, and no less urgent and vital. I wanted to be a part of it and I had a tremendous sense of letdown.

"Oh, Eddie," I said to the infant sleeping on my shoulder, "your life is so simple. You get what you want when you want it, and you make us all happy with a smile. No one even says no to you."

In answer, a little tremor ran through his body and a small sound escaped him.

Suddenly, I had time on my hands. I did a load of baby clothes and cleaned up around the house. Over lunch, I read the paper. The phone rang, and after I had explained for the third time that I was not in need of a stockbroker, I hung up and saw my open notebook. Harlow Sugar. The man from *Cool Times* had said he had once seen D.D. Butler with the man with the odd name.

I took out the Manhattan phone book and looked up Sugar. To my surprise, there were several entries, but there was only one Harlow. I dialed.

"Yeah," a man's voice answered.

"Mr. Sugar?"

"Right here."

"My name is Christine Bennett. I'm trying to find a friend of yours, D.D. Butler."

"D.D., yeah. She moved."

"Then you know her."

"Known her for years. Longer than that even."

"Do you know where she's from?" I asked, picking up my pen.

"I don't understand. First you want to know where she's moved to, now you want to know where she's from. Which is it?"

"Where she's from. Before she lived on the Lower East Side."

"You mind telling me what this is about?"

"Mr. Sugar, are you D.D.'s friend?"

"I'm her friend, yeah. I've known D.D. since she was maybe twenty. Does that qualify me?"

"It does, yes. Mr. Sugar, something very bad has happened to D.D."

"Go on," he said, his voice low.

"She died. Her body was found in a town up the Hudson."

"What the hell is going on here?" he said excitedly. "Who are you? You call me out of the blue, you ask me a bunch of crazy questions, you tell me D.D.'s dead. Where did you get my name from? What's your business?"

"I got your name from Billy Luft at *Cool Times* magazine."

"Never heard of him."

"He said he met you once with D.D."

"Oh, that one. Yeah, I met him once. Guy wears his shirt open down to the navel and has six yards of gold chains around his neck. I know who you mean. Who are you?"

"It's complicated."

"I didn't think it was simple. I'm listening."

"My name is Chris, Chris Bennett. Someone I know disappeared around New Year's Eve. I started looking for her and the trail led up the Hudson to an old house. D.D.'s body was there."

"Not your friend's."

"Not my friend's. But I know there's a connection between D.D. and the young woman I was looking for."

"And the creep at *Cool Times* gave you my name and you thought I could help."

"Yes. I just found out D.D.'s name yesterday. I know nothing at all about who she is, where she's from, why anyone would want to kill her."

"Kill her? You said she was dead. You didn't say someone killed her."

"Someone killed her."

He mumbled an obscenity under his breath. "So what you're really looking for is who killed her."

"That's right."

"I couldn't help you there. She was a nice enough gal. She lived on a shoestring, but I don't think she ever stiffed anyone."

"If I could find her family, Mr. Sugar. Do you know where she's from? Where she went to school? Any place she worked for for a period of time?"

"She worked for an insurance company for a couple of years back in the eighties, maybe the early nineties, but they left town and she didn't go with them. I don't remember where they are now. But I know where she's from because I took her home once and stayed over. It wasn't up the Hudson, I can tell you that."

"You remember where it was?"

"Some town in New Jersey. Wait a minute. I'll think of it, I'll think of it."

I almost held my breath.

"How does Paramus sound?"

I never know how to answer questions like that. "Is that where her folks lived?"

"Yeah. Not too far from the bridge."

"You remember her father's first name?"

"Nope."

"How did she get along with her parents?"

"How does anyone get along with their folks?"

"Does that mean she didn't get along?"

"It means she got along OK. She worked at it. They were nice people, a little old, maybe. Made it hard to relate to them. But they were OK."

"Mr. Sugar, why did D.D. leave New York and go upstate?"

"For peace and quiet. Why does anyone?"

"Was she working on something? Writing a book? Composing a symphony?"

"I like that," he said with a little laugh. "You got a sense of humor. I think maybe she was writing something. She had a story published once. Kinda dark but interesting. She's a person who could be by herself. She didn't need a crowd to get something done. She liked the insurance company, don't get me wrong, but she wanted to write."

"I understand she also took pictures that were published."

"She was a multitalented woman."

I wasn't sure if that was a joke. "You said she had a

story published. Do you know where I could find a copy?"

"I got it right here. I'll put a copy in the mail today if you give me an address."

I gave it to him.

"You'll have it Monday."

"Thank you, Mr. Sugar. I appreciate your help."

"My pleasure."

16

Now I really had a problem. I knew who D.D. Butler's family was and knew more or less where to find them, but I didn't want to be the one to tell them their daughter was dead. It was too late today to do anything anyway. Eddie would be up soon and after his two o'clock feeding, he tended to stay awake. He hadn't been out yet today, so I thought a little walk in the brisk cold would do us both good. But before Eddie woke up, I decided to see whether we had a phone book that included Paramus.

We keep the books of the five boroughs and the Westchester area that we live in downstairs, but Jack has other directories that he stores in the study on the second floor. I went up and opened the closet, where a stack of phone books lay piled on the floor. The third one down was Bergen County, New Jersey.

There was a column and a half of Butlers, but to my amazement only four of them lived in Paramus. I copied them down and finished just as my son made his first sounds.

It was about three when we finally got outside. The driveway was clear of snow and I was able to push the carriage down to the curb, where it took a little work to get it over the mound of frozen snow. Once in the street, walking was a breeze. Oakwood, happily, is a town with good services. On nights when it snows we're often awakened by the sound of snowplows going down the street, but the knowledge that we won't be snowed in makes up for the loss of sleep. I chatted with a couple of neighbors who were also out with their young children and circled our long block slowly, talking to Eddie, who was watching me as his cheeks grew redder. When I got back to the house, I saw Mel's car in her driveway but decided against barging in. Now that she was teaching full-time, her afternoons were very busy and I empathized with her need to be with her children and the myriad tasks that home and family engendered.

"Let's go home, Eddie," I said to my wide-eyed son. And I worked the carriage over the ice and pushed it up the driveway.

The four names and phone numbers were sitting next to the telephone. I put Eddie on the kitchen table in his seat where he could watch me and called the first one on the list.

A woman answered.

"Mrs. Butler?" I asked.

"Yes."

"Is D.D. there?"

"Who?"

"D.D. Butler. Isn't this her number?"

"It's Butler, but there's no D.D. here."

"Thank you." And crossed it off my list.

The second was a child, and I sensed from the first word that this was the wrong number but I asked anyway.

"Who?" she said.

"D.D.," I repeated. "D.D. Butler."

"My name's Sharon."

"Is D.D. there?"

"I don't know D.D."

I thanked her and hung up. The third call was answered by a woman. I asked my question again.

"You want D.D.?"

"Yes, please."

"I haven't heard from D.D. for some time. Are you a friend of hers?"

"I've met her," I said uncomfortably.

"Well, she went to live up in New England, New Hampshire or someplace like that, back in the summer and I haven't heard from her for a while. She called at Christmas, but that's a couple of weeks ago."

"Oh, so she calls from time to time."

"Once in a while. But I can't give you a number. She doesn't have a phone where she's living. And she can't even get mail delivered, though I'm not sure why. Can I help you in any way?"

"Mrs. Butler, could I come out and talk to you?"

"To me? Why would you want to talk to me?"

"Just for a little while. Maybe tomorrow," I said, avoiding the question.

"Well, I suppose I'll be here. Who did you say you were?"

"My name is Chris Bennett. Can I come around one o'clock?"

"Yes, why don't you," she said.

Which meant I would have to deliver the news, but when I thought about it, I decided it was better coming from me than from a police officer.

I told the whole story to Jack at dinner. It was Friday, so he came home at a reasonable hour and we ate together.

"I can see you're upset about Arnold," he said. "You

shouldn't take this personally. If he's representing a client, he has to do everything he can to protect her."

"I know and I explained it all to myself in easy-to-understand terms but it still hurts. Jack, he obviously thinks Susan is guilty."

"Not necessarily. He may know there's a piece of evidence that could make it look bad for her and there's no easy way to work around it. You know the old story of the guy who could clear himself of a murder charge by admitting he spent the night with another woman. He's damned if he does and damned if he doesn't."

I didn't accept his explanation. Arnold was too smart. He had to know something devastating about Susan, and what else could it be except murder? "Anyway," I said, "I talked to this man Harlow Sugar, who led me to D.D. Butler's family. I'm going over there tomorrow, and I'll tell her mother that D.D. is dead."

"You sure you want to do this?"

"I don't want to, but what's the alternative? I think it's better than to have a cop come to her door. Or get a call from the Bladesville people. They're not exactly models of sensitivity."

He smiled. "Good point."

"This Harlow Sugar said that D.D. was writing something. Teddy Toledo told me about some things D.D. got published. If she was up there working on a book, I wonder where it was. You didn't hear about a manuscript, did you?"

"Maybe she finished it and sent it off to a publisher."

"Maybe the killer took it with him."

"Or her."

"Yes."

"Maybe," Jack said, warming to the subject, "it was one of those novels about real people where they change the names so it sounds like fiction but the originals recognize themselves."

"A roman à clef."

"And the original of one of the characters had a New Year's Eve date with D.D."

That ended in murder. "I forgot to tell you. D.D. lied to her mother. She said she was going to New England. The Hudson River valley in New York State hardly qualifies as New England. The mother said, 'New Hampshire or someplace like that.'"

"Maybe she didn't want them coming after her. If they live in New Jersey, chances are they have a car. It wouldn't take long for them to drive up to Bladesville."

"True. They might be disappointed to see the conditions she was living in."

"Or they could drop in at the wrong moment," Jack said, more to the point. "She had no phone. They couldn't call and tell her they were coming."

"Spoil whatever she was planning," I said. "I'll take Eddie with me tomorrow, Jack. Let you get some work done."

"I don't mind watching him."

"You sure?"

"I'm sure. I kinda like to have a day at home with my son."

I was glad to hear it.

Paramus turned out to be a town of some size, filled with New York–style department stores and lots of pretty houses on quiet streets. Jack and I had figured out an easy route for me, and I reached the house just about when I had promised. I was pretty sure the Butlers hadn't been informed of D.D.'s death. Jack had phoned in her name to the Brooklyn precinct detective squad yesterday, but all he had known at that point was the name. Someone would have called the Bladesville sheriff's department by now, but I didn't think they would have located D.D.'s family. If she had no police record, she was just an anonymous human being who had dropped out.

I left the car in front of the bi-level house and went up to the door. A thin, gray-haired woman in glasses opened the door and looked me over.

"I'm Christine Bennett," I said. "Mrs. Butler?" I offered my hand and she shook it. "We spoke yesterday."

"Come in."

We went up four or five steps to the main level, turned left, and went into the living room. It was a large room, with the section at the back of the house used as a dining room. We sat, I feeling as uncomfortable as she looked.

"You wanted to talk to me?" she said.

"I have some things to tell you. It started on New Year's Eve." I went through the story quickly, culminating with my discovery of the body. She sat rigidly, listening and frowning deeply. "We believe the body in that house is your daughter," I said finally.

She shook her head. "No. That's not my daughter. My daughter's in New Hampshire. She called me from there. She told me she was living in an old house that had no phone. She had to go into town to use a pay phone. D.D.'s not in New York State. She's in New England. You've got the wrong person."

I made a decision not to push it. Eventually, someone with official standing would come up her walk and give her the news, and when that happened, she would know it was true and she would have suffered half the pain already. "Perhaps that's so," I said gently. "Can you tell me why D.D. went to New England?"

"How could it be her?" the woman said. "She just called me from New Hampshire for Christmas."

"I don't know," I said.

"She went there to write. She's a very talented girl. She's been published, you know."

"I heard."

"Very talented. She's had a story published. And a magazine printed a whole lot of her pictures, pictures of very important people. D.D. met them all. She knew them. John Kennedy, Junior was one of them. It's a wonderful picture."

"It must be. What was she going to write in New Hampshire?"

"It was a play. She had it all worked out. She would tell me, 'Mom, I finished another scene. I have just a few more to go.' She was in good health. Why would she die? Why would she die in New York when she went to live in New Hampshire?"

I knew that she understood that what I had told her was true, that she was working it out, getting around to believing it, trying to argue against it logically when it wasn't a matter of logic at all; it was a matter of fact. "Did you ever read any of the scenes of D.D.'s play?" I asked.

"No. She kept it to herself. She didn't like to show things around till she finished them."

"What kind of play was it going to be? A drama? A love story?"

"I think it was a murder mystery," she said.

"That sounds exciting," I said, feeling chilled.

The door opened downstairs and a girl's voice called, "Hi, Mom. We're here."

"That's my other daughter," Mrs. Butler said. "Let's not talk about this any more." She got up and went to the stairs. "How's my little lover?" she crooned as a toddler climbed up the last step on his hands and knees, then stood shakily to kiss his grandmother.

He was followed by a pretty, young woman who said, "Oh, hi," as she saw me.

"I'm Chris Bennett. Hello. That's a beautiful little boy you have."

"Oh, thanks. He's a handful. I'm Heather Williams."

"The lady's just going, Heather."

"I'll walk her out, Mom. You stay with Grandma, honey, OK?" she said to her little one.

I followed her down the stairs. Outside she said, "Mom told me someone was coming to ask about my sister. Is something wrong?"

"I believe so. Your mother doesn't believe it."

"Mom never believes bad news. Is something wrong with D.D.? Has there been an accident?"

"I think she's dead, Heather."

"Oh, God. I knew it. I knew it when Mom called." She was trying to hold herself together. "Are you a friend of hers?"

"I'm a friend of someone else who disappeared on New Year's Eve. I went looking for her and found a body. I thought it was hers but it may be your sister's."

"In New Hampshire, right?"

"No, in a town called Bladesville, New York. It's up the Hudson."

"Mom said D.D. was in New Hampshire."

"I can't explain the discrepancies."

"Look, I have to go inside. Can I call you?"

"I wish you would." I wrote down the necessary information and handed it to her. "I'm home most of the time. I have a new baby."

She smiled a little and said, "Congratulations. I'll try to call tomorrow."

The door opened and her mother came outside, carrying the little boy. "Come in, Heather. It's cold out here."

"Mrs. Butler," I said, "did D.D. tell you whether her play was finished yet?"

"It wasn't," her mother said. "I asked her when she called at Christmas. She said it would be finished by New Year's Eve."

"Wow," Jack said when I finished my story. "I'd like to get hold of that manuscript."

"So would I. But who knows if there even was a manuscript? This D.D. sounds like a strange person. She makes her own rules, says what suits her purposes."

"She must have loved her mother," Jack said. "She called her."

"I hope I hear from Heather. She knows things."

"You have a problem with my calling in what I know to the precinct squad in Brooklyn?"

"No, go ahead. The sooner they positively identify D.D. the better it'll be for her family. It's probably too late to find prints at the Butler's home but maybe they have some of her possessions that'll yield a match."

"Her mother'll know the dentist D.D. saw."

"Right. Go make your call. I'll entertain our son for a while."

17

"The bottom line is they're not too interested." Jack sat down next to me and picked up Eddie. "Their missing person is back and she's a suspect in a homicide upstate. That's what they care about. And the detective in charge of the case is off today. So I told the guy who answered what I knew, and maybe it'll get up to Bladesville and maybe it won't."

"I hope it does. I want that poor woman put out of her misery."

I also wanted a call from Heather Williams. With a last name like hers and no clue as to where she lived, I had no chance of finding her without her mother's help, and I was sure Mrs. Butler would not give it. I was convinced, as I had been several times before when looking into a murder, that something in the life of Delilah Donna Butler would give me the key to her death. There had to be a reason why a young woman who had worked for an established company for two years, and presumably enjoyed it if I could believe Harlow Sugar, would give up a reliable income, friends, and relatives, and move to a lonely house where the only transportation was provided by a friend who lived in another town; why she would lie about where she was; why she would dedicate herself to a project that might or might not pay her. She had taken the house for six months. Was that because she thought she would be finished with her project, the play, in six months? Or was that when she thought her funds would run out?

The hoped-for call from Heather did not come on Saturday. Jack made a great fire Saturday night and turned on a movie on television. It held my interest for a while but about the time he fell asleep, I started to think about D.D. and what her mother had said. The play would be finished by New Year's Eve. The last scene would be written by New Year's Eve. Everything hinged on New Year's Eve.

The movie ended and I heard a cry from upstairs. I put my hand over Jack's and he woke up.

"Huh?"

"I'm going to nurse Eddie. He didn't get the girl."

"Who? Eddie?"

"The guy in the movie."

"I didn't think he would." He rubbed his eyes.

"Jack, I have a feeling about the D.D. Butler case. I don't think she was writing a play at all. I think she was writing, or composing, a scenario for murder."

"Whose?"

"I don't know. But I think her intended victim turned the tables on her."

But I didn't have a clue as to who D.D.'s intended victim was. It couldn't have been Teddy Toledo if she told him not to drop by over New Year's Eve weekend. Unless he lied, which he would have if he wanted to protect himself. Susan was the only person who we knew for sure had visited the farmhouse before me, but that didn't make her a killer. And why would D.D. want to kill Susan, assuming my theory of the murder was correct?

I took my cousin Gene to mass on Sunday morning

and brought him back to the house so he could get to know his newest cousin.

"He's little," Gene said, as we stood over the crib together.

"He's very little. But he grows bigger every day. He weighs about ten pounds now."

"Wow!" Gene said. "Ten pounds."

"But he's cute, isn't he?"

"Yeah. He's cute."

"Do you want to touch him?"

"Uh-huh." Gene stroked Eddie's little cheek with one finger. Then he turned and smiled at me. "That feels nice."

"He has very smooth, soft skin, doesn't he?"

"Smooth," Gene repeated. "Is he one year old?"

"No, he's just six weeks old. Almost seven weeks."

"Wow," Gene said. "Seven weeks old."

"Sit on the chair, Gene. I'll put him in your lap. Be very careful, OK?"

"OK."

I took Eddie out of the crib and laid him in Gene's big lap. They spent a minute looking at each other. Gene was smiling. "I think he likes me," he said.

"I know he likes you. He knows you're his cousin and he knows you're a very good person."

Suddenly Eddie began to cry.

"He's mad at me," Gene said.

"No, he's not. He's just hungry. When babies don't know what else to do, they cry."

"Take him away, Kix."

"Here we go." I lifted the baby off his lap. "Why don't you go downstairs and help Jack with dinner. I'll be down in a little while."

He was glad to go.

* * *

The call from Heather Williams came late in the afternoon, after I had taken Gene back to Greenwillow.

"I'm glad you called," I said, understating how I felt.

"I just got home. The police came today to talk to Mom and Dad. They want dental records and pictures and things. No one can understand why D.D. was in New York State when she told us she was in New Hampshire. Unless it isn't D.D."

"They should be able to determine that pretty soon with the dental records," I said. "Can you tell me how old D.D. was?"

"Thirty-one."

"Were you close?"

"Well, we're close in age, so we grew up together and we were always best friends."

"But you hadn't seen her recently, had you?"

"No. She went away last summer and I haven't seen her since. I guess maybe we stopped being best friends when I got married. She wasn't angry or anything; it's just that our lives went in different directions. D.D.'s work was very important to her and my husband was first in my life."

"I understand. Did she tell you she was going away?"

"She called me one night in the summer. She said she had a little money saved and she had things she wanted to do, so she was going up to New England for a few months."

"Did she tell you about this play she was writing?"

"No, she didn't. She told that to Mom. She told me she had things she had to work out, some problems she wanted to solve. She said she'd be back when it was all taken care of."

"Did she ever call you?"

"She called Mom. Once I was in the house when she

called and we talked a little. I asked her for her number so we could call her back and save her some money, but she wouldn't give it."

That was because D.D. wasn't in the area code she claimed to be in. "Do you know any of D.D.'s friends, Heather?"

"Not anymore. When we were going through school I did. When she went to New York to work, I kinda lost track of them."

"Did she ever mention a Susan Stark?"

"It doesn't sound familiar."

"Did she ever tell you about someone she disliked, maybe even hated?"

"Well—uh-oh, just a minute." There were some sounds and then Heather came back. "I'm sorry, I've got to go. My mother's on the other line."

"Heather, may I have your number?"

"Sure." She said it quickly, then, "G'bye," and hung up.

I wasn't sure whether staying on the phone longer would have yielded more. People don't often tell their friends and sisters who they're planning to do away with. At least Brooklyn had notified Bladesville, and Bladesville had gotten the Paramus police to notify the Butlers.

But I was stuck. I had learned a tremendous amount, had traced D.D. to the farmhouse and then worked backward to her family, more than the police had done. But I had failed to find a connection between her and Susan, and Susan was now off-limits. And without that connection, I had no idea which way to turn.

Monday morning I did something I had not done before. I drove over to the post office early in the morning and asked for my mail. It wasn't completely

sorted yet, but when I saw the large envelope from
Harlow Sugar, I knew I had what I wanted.

At home I put Eddie where he could watch me and I
opened the envelope and pulled out several badly copied
sheets. Many lines were too black to be legible but it
didn't matter; there was enough to make it worthwhile.

The story was titled "Lists" and it was unlike any story
I had ever read before.

I am a writer of lists. My lists keep me going. Without
them there is no plan to my day and no reason for my
being. There is nothing ordinary about my lists. My
list of the people I hate is not very long but it is sincere. The list of people I love is much longer but it is
also less honest. At the top of the sincere list is my Big
Boss. At the bottom of the insincere list is my
boyfriend Todd. Between those names stretches my
entire history.

It was a chilling story. In it the narrator, a woman
bursting with hatred and resentment, plans to kill not
someone on the list of people she hates, but someone on
the other list, the people she loves. She picks the person
almost at random, weighing the pros and cons of all the
people on the list. In the end she kills a stranger, from her
description a young man without a mean bone in his body.

It was a terribly depressing story. Since it was the only
one Harlow Sugar had sent me, I couldn't tell what the
contents of the rest of the magazine were like. Perhaps
this was the kind of writing they liked, but it wasn't my
style, and while I felt deeply sorry for the young man
who eventually is marked for death, I had sad feelings,
too, for the narrator. Although strongly motivated to do
evil, she betrayed in herself a wisp of humanity here and

there, a hand extended in a void. She struck me as wounded and hurt.

I set the story aside, feeling troubled. "Almost time for breakfast, isn't it, Eddie?" I said to get myself back into a world of feeling and compassion.

I put the story out of my head while Eddie nursed and didn't think about D.D. till he was sleeping happily in his crib. I had no way of knowing whether D.D. herself had a boyfriend—Heather hadn't mentioned one—or if the story was entirely fictional or partly true. Would a person planning a murder publish her intentions?

I was getting ready to put lunch together when the doorbell rang. When I opened the door, no one was there. Suddenly, from around the side of the house a young woman appeared.

"Hi," she said.

"Hello."

"You must be Chris. I'm Susan Stark."

I said, "Susan," and a chill went through me as I put the face together with the picture Ada had given me.

"Arnold doesn't know I'm here. He'd kill me if he knew I was talking to you. Can I come in?"

I was scared. It was the first confirmation I had that I believed she was guilty, or at least that Arnold believed it. My baby was upstairs in his crib. A lot of what-ifs ran through my mind, none of them very pleasant.

"Just for a few minutes," Susan said, when I didn't respond. "I know I should have called first, but this seemed the best way."

"Sure," I said. I opened the door for her and took her coat when she was inside. "Let's go into the family room."

She looked a little different from her picture, maybe a bit older and more tired. "This is a nice room." She smiled at me disarmingly.

"We just built it a few months ago."

"Chris, I heard about you from my mother and talked to Arnold about you. He doesn't want you digging into this case because he's afraid of what it'll turn up. Or that's what he says. But I'm completely innocent and nothing you find out can hurt me. I think it can only help."

"Let's talk about it." I was on my guard, but her manner was persuasive. Maybe she just wanted to find out what I knew and determine whether it could hurt her. One thing was sure. I wanted her out of here before Eddie awoke about two hours from now.

"I know that you found the farmhouse and D.D. Butler's body. I'm not sure how you managed it, but Arnold said you were good. I was in that house on New Year's Eve—Arnold said they found my prints there so I can't lie about it—but D.D. was dead when I got there."

"Why were you visiting her?"

Susan smiled. "It wasn't exactly a social call. D.D.'s life was mixed up in mine and I wanted to talk to her. I think that her path and mine crossed somewhere. I think she knew who I was and she was—I don't know how to put this—she was infiltrating herself into my life."

"Just a minute." I got up and went to the kitchen to get my notebook and a pen. "Where do you think your paths crossed, Susan?" I asked, when I was sitting again.

"I'm not sure. I've tried very hard to think of a time and place. I may have met her at a party a couple of years ago. There were a lot of people there and there was a girl or woman who asked me a lot of questions. But I'm not sure."

"And how was she infiltrating herself into your life?"

"I think she actually got me my job."

She was perfectly serious. "How could she do that?" I asked.

"I never applied for that job. I got a phone call from someone who asked me to come in for an interview. It sounded great so I went. They got my name from someone but they never said who. I think it was D.D., although she may have covered up who she was."

"How did the others get their jobs? How did Jill?"

"There was an ad in the *Times*."

"But you never saw the ad."

"Never."

"Do you think she remained involved with your work?"

"No. I think she got me the job and then pulled back."

"You know this sounds crazy."

"I know. But it's true."

"How did you find out her name, Susan?"

"It's a little hard to explain and I don't want to get anyone in trouble. Let's just say I had a source."

"Teddy?" I asked.

She looked blank.

"Was he your source?"

"I don't know a Teddy."

"How did you learn about the farmhouse then?" I asked.

"D.D. wrote to me with the address."

"When was this?"

"About three weeks ago."

I shook my head. "You told Mrs. Halliday about Bladesville more than three weeks ago."

"Mrs. Halliday," she said, as though she now understood the source of my information. "Yes, you're right. I did tell her before I got that letter. Actually, when I found out D.D.'s name, I looked her up in the phone book. She was listed but she wasn't living there anymore. I went down and talked to a neighbor of hers. She's the one who told me that D.D. had moved to Bladesville."

"And when did you talk to this neighbor?" I was full of skepticism, which I hoped didn't show.

"A couple of months ago. I told Mrs. Halliday after that."

"Would you excuse me for a minute?"

"Sure."

I went to the kitchen, pulled out the Manhattan directory, and carried it to where I knew Susan couldn't see me. I looked up Butler. There were columns of them but there was no Delilah, no Donna, no D period, D period. If Susan had found D.D.'s address and phone number in the phone book, it wasn't in this one, and there was no other that I could think of. She was telling me lies, lots of them.

18

I returned to the family room with two glasses of Coke and handed one to Susan.

"Gee, thanks. I really need that."

I waited till we had drunk some. I was getting hungry and I needed another glass of milk, but I was nervous enough about Susan's presence that I didn't want to drink milk and tip her off that I had a baby in the house. "Do you have D.D's letter with you?" I asked finally.

"No."

"Where did she address it to?"

"At work. She knew where I worked. I'm not sure she knew where I was living."

That, at least, made sense. If you steer someone to a job, you know her work address. "What did the letter say?"

"She said she wanted to meet me. That she knew about me and thought I'd be interested in meeting her."

"Did she say when she wanted to see you?"

"New Year's Eve. Not at night. She said it was too dark at night. I didn't understand what she meant till I got there. She said to come during the day."

"Did she say anyone else would be there?"

She gave me a quizzical look. "No, she didn't. Why do you ask?"

"Because if you didn't kill D.D., someone else did. I wondered if this was some kind of reunion."

She looked troubled, or perhaps just thoughtful. "Someone else was obviously there before me, but I don't know if he was invited. For all I know it may have been a drifter who knocked on the door."

"I don't believe that, Susan. I've been to that farmhouse. It's not near anything. You'd need a car to get there."

"D.D. didn't have a car."

"How do you know?"

"I didn't see one."

"D.D. had a friend," I said. "He picked her up and took her into town so she could shop."

"Then maybe he's the one."

"It's possible."

"You aren't telling me much, Chris. I really need your help. I left my fingerprints all over that house, and nobody else did. I'm the only person they can link to the house, and I'm the only living person who knows I was there after the murder. Except for the murderer."

"You're keeping so much from me," I said. I looked down at my notes. "You've told me almost nothing I didn't know before. Except that D.D. may have gotten you your job interview and that she sent you a letter a couple of weeks ago. What was her interest in you? What was your interest in her? How did all this get started? If I'm going to help you, I have to know these things."

"Other people's lives are involved. I want you to take what I tell you on faith. Arnold said you—"

"Arnold didn't tell you I take facts on faith. I need to know your connection to D.D. Butler. Am I to believe that she met you at a party and decided to run your life?"

"It wasn't exactly like that."

"Maybe she knew before the party that you would be there."

"It's possible," she said hesitantly.

"And that's why she was there."

She let her breath out. "It probably wasn't a coincidence that we were both there at the same time," she admitted.

"I'm struggling to make sense of this. Tell me about your visit to the farmhouse."

"I got there before eleven."

"Where did you spend the night before?"

"At my parents' in Brooklyn." She said it so casually, it was hard to believe it had been such a big issue.

"Did you see your parents before you left?"

She looked at me suspiciously. "I'm not sure."

"Go on about the visit."

"I got there. I left the car in the driveway and went to the front door. There was a doorbell but it didn't work. I realized afterward that there wasn't any electricity. So I called. There was no answer. I knocked and then I opened the door."

"It wasn't locked?"

"It couldn't have been or I wouldn't have gotten in. I went inside and called her name. I called it a lot of times."

"Was it warm inside, Susan?" I asked.

She thought about it. "Maybe not when I first went in, but it was warmer when I got near the kitchen."

Then she must have been killed that morning, I thought, or late the night before. The fire in the kitchen stove couldn't have lasted many hours without additional fuel. "What rooms did you walk through?"

"The dining room, I think. There wasn't much furniture so it was hard to tell, but I went through it and I got to the kitchen."

"What did you see?"

She pressed her lips together. "I didn't see her at first. The light coming in was very bright and it took a few seconds for my eyes to adjust. Then I saw the stove and the old cabinets with glass fronts and the dishes on the shelves. I saw all the windows at the back, looking out on the fields and a couple of trees. It was like a quick slide show, if you know what I mean, a glimpse of this and a glimpse of that. And then I saw her. She looked sort of—" She stopped, a look of pain on her face.

"Tell me exactly what you saw. Try to recall every detail, Susan. Each one might be part of the solution."

"A person lying face-down. Blue jeans. Maybe a sweatshirt, I'm not sure. Hair, kind of messy." She was looking away, seeing it as she spoke. "Blood. Blood on the hair, blood on the floor."

"Did you touch her?"

"No." It was the loudest syllable she had uttered since her arrival.

"Did you touch anything else? Did you look around?"

"I was frozen when I saw her. I said her name a couple of times but she didn't move. I kind of backed away. You know, I may have reached out and held onto something to steady myself, a cabinet or a counter or something. I felt a little dizzy or light-headed, and my stomach didn't feel too great. Then I just turned around and got out of there."

"When you were coming in, did you notice whether there was a door between the dining room and the kitchen?"

"There could have been but I didn't notice."

"Then you didn't open a door to get to the kitchen?"

"No. I'm sure of that. I just walked from one room into the other."

"And the kitchen was warm."

"Definitely. Not hot but I could feel the difference when I went in. You know what? I heard a sound—sounds—in the kitchen and I realized they were coming from the woodstove. Not loud, but a little crackling."

"That's very interesting," I said.

"I see what you're driving at," she said with excitement. "D.D. couldn't have been dead very long, could she? She must have put wood on the fire if it was still warm and crackling."

"And the door should have been closed. If you heat one room, you keep the door closed to keep the heat inside."

"Was it closed when you got there?" she asked.

"It was open."

"I didn't open it. The killer must have left it open when he walked out of the kitchen."

Why not? I thought. He had no reason to care about the comfort of the person he left behind. If he gave the matter any thought at all, he would have known that he would be better off if the body froze quickly. There would be no smell to attract animal life.

"Did you look around the house, Susan? Before or after you found the body?"

"No. When I went in, I was looking for D.D. When I left, I really needed some fresh air. I was scared and sick to my stomach."

"When you drove up on the property, did you see tire tracks?"

"I wasn't looking for tire tracks. I was looking for a place to drive up, a driveway or a road. There was a place near the house where the snow was tamped down so I drove up on it."

And we, of course, had driven over the accumulated tracks a couple of days later. "Did you see anyone around?"

"No one. I just ran like hell."

"Why didn't you report finding the body?" I asked.

"I know, and why didn't I come home? I was scared. I had this crazy feeling that D.D. had arranged this."

"Arranged her death?"

"In a way, yes. I was sure she'd been involved in getting me my job. I felt she was manipulating me, setting me up. What if that wasn't D.D. lying on the floor in the kitchen? Maybe it was someone else. What if D.D. had killed her and was long gone, leaving me to look like a killer?"

"But why would anyone think you killed some stranger in that farmhouse?"

"I couldn't explain why I was there. I couldn't explain why I had gone, who D.D. was, what was going on. I just had to get away and think."

"Where did you go?"

"I drove around. I found a motel. I had some money with me because I'd cashed a check before the weekend, so I didn't have to use a credit card. I got food at a supermarket. I had promised Jill I'd have her car back by Monday so I drove to Brooklyn after a couple of nights and left the car."

"Where did you stay after that?"

"I went to an old friend I could trust who I knew from college. She lives in New Jersey. I took a bus out there after I returned the car."

"And what made you come back?"

"I was living in limbo. I have a life, a job, Kevin, my

parents. I knew they would be worried sick. And I didn't want to lose my job. I love it."

The statement came across as honest and sincere, unlike some of the other things she had said. "Have you seen Kevin?" I asked.

"I talked to him. I haven't seen him yet. I went to my parents' and they called Arnold, and he said not to talk to anyone. I just told Kevin I was back and I would see him when I could."

"Susan, did you take anything from that farmhouse?"

"Nothing, I swear it. I was so scared, so confused, I just turned and ran."

"Because whatever was used to kill D.D. isn't in the house. And there's no pocketbook, no wallet, no ID of any kind."

"Then the killer took it. I didn't. I told you, I didn't even know if that was D.D. lying there."

I looked at my watch. "I'm really out of time," I said. "I'm willing to help you, but first you have to tell me what you're withholding. You know what it is. There's a huge gap in your story. Fill it in and I'll help you. And please call next time before you come." I felt a little heartless saying it but if I were going to see Susan again in my home, maybe I would drop Eddie off first. I was inclined to believe that she was telling the truth as far as she went, that she hadn't killed D.D. Butler, but something about her made me nervous. Maybe it was her own nervousness, her lack of complete truthfulness.

She said, "OK," her voice and her face subdued. "There is one other thing I haven't told you. It's about Kevin." She looked very troubled.

"What is it?"

"I think D.D. arranged that, too. My meeting with Kevin. I think she had me all sized up. She put us together because she knew it would work. And the crazy thing is she was right. I love him."

I gave her her coat, and she left me to eat my lunch and ponder her last revelation.

19

By the time Jack came home that night, I had already called Joseph and arranged to drive up to St. Stephen's the following day. Except for Joseph, none of the nuns had seen Eddie, and I knew they wanted to. Jack and I had been married at St. Stephen's but when Eddie was born, my mother-in-law's choice for the location of the baptism prevailed. We had it at Jack's old church in Brooklyn, and only Joseph came down to join us. So this was a good opportunity to show off my beautiful son and get the benefit of Joseph's discerning point of view in a case where she had actually seen the crime scene.

"You think the nuns'll spoil Eddie rotten?" Jack asked as he ate his late dinner.

"Probably. He deserves that once in a while, don't you think? We're both such tough parents."

"Tough, yeah. Gets me wondering about those abuse cases we keep hearing about, how the hell people do it."

"I know."

"OK, tell me about the case. Susan herself turned up on your doorstep. That must have been a shock."

"It was. I wasn't sure whether to let her in or not, but I did."

"And she didn't tell you enough to put your finger on a killer or you wouldn't be going up to St. Stephen's tomorrow."

"That's about it," I said. "She told me some interesting stuff but she left out a lot." I filled him in on the pluses and minuses as he ate.

"She thinks this woman steered her into a job and a relationship? It's eerie and I can't see a reason for it. Both those things turned out well. Made Susan happy."

"That's right."

"So it doesn't look like there was any evil intent. But what's the purpose? What did D.D. Butler get out of it?"

"Maybe she was going to get something out of it on New Year's Eve."

"And it backfired," Jack said.

"But not with Susan," I reminded him. "With someone else."

"You think she was a one-woman do-good organization? And one of her missions went sour?"

"I don't know. I'm hoping Joseph comes up with something. Let me tell you who I'd like to talk to even though I know I won't be able to: I've never laid eyes on Susan's father. Remember New Year's Day when we were all going nuts trying to figure out where Susan was? Her father went to his office because, we were told, when he's worried, he likes to work. I wonder how he spent New Year's Eve."

"Good point."

"And when I asked Susan where she had spent the night before New Year's Eve—you remember the discussions about whether she was home and they just didn't see her or whether she disappeared from her doorstep when Kevin dropped her off—she said, as though it was the most unimportant question she'd ever been asked, that she'd spent the night at her parents'. That really bothers me. Even if her bedroom was around a corner—and it is; I saw it—don't you hear a toilet flushing or a shower running?"

"I think the Starks said, or at least her mother did since no one's talked to her father—that they were out that day, that Susan could have gotten up earlier or later and left without being seen. If it was later, they wouldn't have heard a shower running."

"I don't like it," I said. "Susan told me she got to the farmhouse before eleven. It was supposedly her first trip up there. It had to take an hour and a half from Brooklyn."

"Easily."

"Looking for roads, driving in unfamiliar territory. I'm uneasy about it," I said. "I'm just wondering if Ada lied to protect Susan. Or to make it a more complicated case."

"Anything's possible."

I looked at my notebook with its underlined unanswered questions. Susan knew about D.D. long before the letter inviting her to Bladesville. How did she know? Why wouldn't she tell me?

"Susan and D.D. connected before the letter Susan admits receiving a few weeks ago inviting her up to Bladesville on New Year's Eve. She won't say what the connection was, whether it was letters or meetings or phone calls. I told her I wouldn't help her unless she gave me the missing information."

"Getting tough, I see."

"Well, I'm the mother of a son. You have to be tough with sons, don't you?"

"Ah," my gun-toting, hard-boiled husband said, "not this year. Maybe when he's put in twelve months."

I leaned over and kissed him, then left the table for a minute. When I came back I handed him the envelope with D.D.'s published short story. "I don't exactly recommend this for bedtime reading, but it may give you some insights into D.D. Butler's character."

He took a quick look at it and put it back in the envelope. I didn't envy him the task of reading it.

"What a downer," he said at breakfast the next morning. "That story. Woman with a dark soul. Can't say I'd visit her in a lonely farmhouse after reading that."

"I doubt whether Susan read it."

"You showing that to Sister Joseph?"

"I don't know." It was something I had thought about. "I can show it to her and she can exercise her own judgment on whether she wants to read it or not."

"Well, say hello to her for me."

I promised I would. Later on in the morning, I packed Eddie into the car and drove to the convent.

Someone had put a pale blue ribbon tied in a huge bow on a stake in front of one of the parking spaces outside the Mother House, and I glided into it with a smile. "Looks like we have a welcoming committee, Eddie," I said, but Eddie was fast asleep. I got him out of the car and slung my bag and his bag over my shoulder and managed to get a grip on the little seat. I didn't have to carry them more than a few steps, because the nuns were on the lookout and three came running to help me. I ended up with only my shoulder bag as everything else, including Eddie, was whisked into the Mother House.

"Chris, you look wonderful," Angela said, as I took my coat off. She had a firm grasp on Eddie, who seemed happy to continue sleeping on her shoulder.

"Not as thin as before."

"Oh, you'll get back. You were never one to sit idle. But what a beautiful baby he is. I hope he wakes up before you leave so I can see the color of his eyes."

"I'm sure he will. Let me get his snowsuit off."

"He's so wonderfully warm," Angela said. "And he smells like an angel."

"You can have him back," I promised.

We carried him up to Joseph's office so she could have a look before we got down to work. I was interested that she seemed very pleased to see him and touch him, but was less enthusiastic about holding him. I had never had much interest in babies myself before I became pregnant. They had been cute and appealing from a distance, but nothing in me had craved the closeness of holding one in my arms.

When the introduction had been completed, Angela took Eddie away and Joseph and I sat at the end of her long table, opposite each other, to eat lunch off the trays that awaited us.

"I've really been on pins and needles waiting to hear from you," she said. "I've seen that kitchen in Bladesville in my dreams."

"So have I."

"I gather from what you said on the phone yesterday that you've come a long way since discovering the body."

"But not all the way. There are huge gaps in what I know and I'm not sure how to fill them in."

"Then let's start at the beginning."

I did in my usual way, referring to my notes, backtracking occasionally, answering a question here and there. I had D.D.'s short story with me, and I handed it across the table as I came near the end of my own story. Joseph slid it out of the envelope and began to read it, her face, which is as clear and smooth and benign as any I have ever seen, wrinkling with distaste.

"Not a very happy woman," she said, setting the story aside.

"It doesn't appear that way, does it?" I finished up

with Susan's surprise appearance and what she had told me.

"Certainly the most interesting things that Susan said concern D.D.'s involvement in her life and the fact that she spent the night before New Year's Eve at her parents'."

"Why is that last so interesting?" I asked, having thought so myself.

"The way you tell it, Susan had no compunctions about admitting she slept at the Starks'. If I interpreted your telling of it correctly, she might actually have said, 'Good morning, Mom,' before she left the house."

"That's just the way it came across to me."

"It's possible that she didn't see them, of course. I wonder if she left a note. Kevin was supposed to pick her up there that afternoon, wasn't he?"

"That evening, I'd guess. He called in the afternoon and she wasn't there."

"Can we account for Susan's father's whereabouts that day?"

"I've never spoken to him, Joseph. I've never laid eyes on him."

"I think you should. He may not grant you an interview but I think you should try to get one. You've talked to everyone else we know about, certainly many more people than the police have, and that's a gaping hole. Perhaps he has nothing to add, but if there's something peculiar about Susan having slept at home that night, he might just drop it accidentally and you would have a juicy bit of information."

"I'll give it a try."

"You know, ideas are swirling around in my mind as we talk, some of them a bit far-fetched, some not quite so. Now that you've spoken to Susan, now that you've learned her admitted connections to D.D. Butler, I think you ought to explore each of them some more. Just ask a simple question of each: Why that particular job? Why Kevin?"

"The job was advertised in the *Times*," I said.

"And D.D. could have heard about it that way. I still think it's a good question to ask."

I know better than to argue. If I could get Kevin to talk to me, to tell me where and how he met Susan, some link might turn up. "I'll give Kevin a call."

"And in all these brain swirlings I keep coming back to the Donaldsons, Farmer Fred and his wife. A woman comes to the door, gives them an obviously false name, and they rent out their condemned farmhouse for six months' rent in cash. Go back over your notes, Chris. Review your recollections of your meeting with that couple. There's something there, I'm sure of it."

"What about Teddy?" I asked.

"Yes, Teddy. Teddy the artist, who has a friend who's a real estate agent. Teddy, who drives D.D. to shop for groceries because she's stuck without a car. Teddy, who is allegedly told not to turn up on New Year's weekend. It could all be true. I think if Teddy killed D.D., we need a motive. To listen to his tale, he's a good friend, a very helpful person. If he got tired of being either, why not just tell her?"

It sounded perfectly reasonable. D.D. could have posed no threat to Teddy; she couldn't get to him without his help. She had obviously not asked the D'Agatis for assistance in getting around. "It's just that Teddy had opportunity, even if we can't think of a motive. He could have gone there at night, turned his car lights off, killed her, and driven away without anyone seeing him."

"Why?"

"I don't know. He said D.D. was planning something. He didn't know what, just a feeling he had. And he said she might have been writing something, as her mother claimed."

"She must have been doing something all those months in that farmhouse." Joseph is one of those people who think that time wasted is life wasted. "Did the police find anything she had written?"

"Nothing."

"Nothing, nothing, nothing. Chris, this young woman had a plan. A couple of people have told you that, and I think they're right. The plan involved having Susan visit on New Year's Eve, possibly having another person visit the same day, possibly not. Find out where Kevin was. Find out where Susan's father was. Think about the Donaldsons. And two other things. D.D. Butler seems to have been a disturbed young woman. Did this happen suddenly, or is there a history that her family is keeping secret? And the other thing is magazines. There seem to be several magazines in this case. You're close now. The more I think about it, the closer I believe you are."

I didn't bother saying I had no idea what she was talking about. "Would you like to finish the story?" I asked.

"Leave it with me for a few minutes. I'll bring it down with me. You have plenty of visiting to do, I'm sure."

I gathered up my notes. "Joseph, I have a question to ask you on a very different subject. If a woman nursed her baby in a car or in a sheltered place outside her home, how do you think the nuns would feel about it?"

The question was clearly a surprise and caught her imagination. She smiled. "I think their feelings would run from negative to, 'Can't you think of something else to complain about?' Have you been trying to formulate a policy for yourself?"

"I nursed Eddie in my car and got hauled to a local police station."

Joseph laughed. "Chris, what a story. I hope you asserted your maternal rights."

"I did, but I didn't have to. New York State has a law protecting me, but the sheriff's deputy was unaware of it."

"I'll bet your husband knew about it."

"And Arnold Gold. They let me go with great embarrassment." I took myself downstairs so she could look at D.D. Butler's story.

I wasn't sure who was entertaining whom. Everybody seemed to be giggling, including Eddie.

"You'd better bring him back when he's old enough to eat my cookies," Sister Dolores, a resident of the Villa, the home for retired nuns, said. "I've got a bag of them for you, but this little one doesn't have the teeth for them yet."

"Or the digestive system," I said. "Thank you for baking." I opened the bag and sniffed, the smell nearly driving me wild. "I'd better lock these in the trunk for the trip home."

"Don't be so quick to leave. It's a beautiful day. You could show your little son around the convent and drop in on the Villa. I know a few people who'd love to say hello."

So we did. And when it came time to nurse him, I found a quiet, empty room and closed the door. After what Joseph had said, I was sure it wouldn't offend her, but I preferred not to find out whom it might upset.

Just before we left, Joseph found me and gave me back the envelope with the story. "It's hard to believe anyone published this," she said. "I may not be a literary critic, but it strikes me as rather trashy."

"I feel the same way."

"But I think there's more to it than that. With hindsight, I think D.D. was playing a little prank, signaling her plans. I wouldn't be surprised if there are useful clues in this story, especially in her lists of people, if you can decipher them."

"I'll certainly try," I said.

Joseph bent and planted a kiss on Eddie's cheek. "Have a safe drive home."

20

There were several messages on the machine when we got back. Heather Williams and Jack had called, among other less important callers. I tried Jack first but he was out of the station house.

Eddie had awakened as the car came to a stop, and he was fussy. I gave him some water but it had a limited effect. I have to admit to being less than calm when my baby cried but I was pretty sure he wasn't hungry and I knew he was dry. I set him up in his baby seat and he watched me, crying intermittently while I called Heather.

"Chris," she said above a background of similar baby noises, "thanks for calling back. I'm sorry I had to run the other day. Mom's been in pretty bad shape, as you can imagine."

"Yes, I can."

"I wanted to tell you something about D.D. I don't know if it's important but I'm sure Mom didn't tell you, because she wouldn't. D.D. was adopted."

"Really," I said.

"Yes. Mom and Dad had been married for a long time and they'd been trying to adopt for years because they couldn't have kids of their own. Eventually, their number came up and they got D.D."

"Was she an infant?"

"I think so. There are slews of pictures of her all

178

wrapped up in baby blankets. They must have gone through a dozen rolls of film right after they got her."

That would explain why Mrs. Butler seemed so much older than usual for the mother of someone in her early thirties. "I really appreciate your telling me this. Your parents must have been luckier the second time around. They got you just a year or two after D.D."

"No, Mom gave birth to me."

"I thought you said—"

"I did, but it was the old story. As soon as D.D. came into their lives, Mom became pregnant. It happens all the time but every time it does, it seems like a miracle. Mom just got pregnant and had me as if there'd never been a problem."

"Amazing. You said the other day, D.D. was your best friend. Did you and D.D. always get along when you were growing up?"

"Sure. She was Big Sister and I was Little Sister. I looked up to her."

"And she? Was there jealousy?"

"I don't think so. I think we were a pretty happy family."

"What about your folks, Heather? Was there any preferential treatment because you were born into the family?"

"Chris, my mother is the most evenhanded, fair person I've ever met. That's why she'll never tell anyone that D.D. was adopted. As far as she's concerned, she has two daughters. That's it."

"And your father?" I asked. She had been pretty specific that she was talking about her mother.

"Well, Dad's kind of a tough guy, and very old-fashioned in a lot of ways. He wanted both of us to go to school and get jobs and get married. D.D. worked for a while but she never stuck with anything for long. And when she quit her last job, Dad really wasn't very happy. They argued about it."

I was thinking about the dark story D.D. had written and her list of people she hated. But just because her father argued with her didn't mean he hated her or even disliked her. He wanted the best for his daughter. "Let me ask you something else. When D.D. was younger, did she ever have problems, you know, behavioral kinds of things?"

I could almost hear her trying to decide what to say. "Mom would never tell you," she began. "But there were some things. A couple of her teachers thought that her writing showed she was disturbed about something. And there were a couple of incidents."

"What kind of incidents?" I prompted.

"She did some very cruel things once to a girl she didn't like, a girl she thought was being nasty to her."

"Was anything done to help D.D.?"

"You mean like counseling? Mom wouldn't hear of it. Mom had two perfect daughters and if one of them acted antisocial, then she must have been provoked."

"But counseling was recommended?"

"I guess you could say so. Someone from the school called Mom. I only heard scraps of conversations so I really can't tell you much more."

"Did D.D. ever try to locate her birth mother, Heather?"

"Never." She said it absolutely. "I even asked her once if she'd thought about it. She said she hadn't. She said she didn't care. It was all the craze, she said, find your birth mother and catch up on the past. She wouldn't have any of it."

"Thank you very much, Heather. This must be a very difficult time for all of you."

"It is, but I want to find out who murdered my sister."

"I'm doing my best," I said.

Altogether it was a lot of new information. It gave me much more to think about: the secret troubles of a child, the relationships that form our lives and can make or break us. Did D.D. resent her adoptive father? I wondered, not for the first time, why he had not been around when I came to visit. Surely his wife had told him I was coming, that I had news about D.D. It was a Saturday, a day that many men spend around the house, but he hadn't been there.

Eddie was sounding very unhappy. I picked him up and started walking, patting his back. He quieted, two fingers going into his mouth. D.D.'s mother and father could surely have had different feelings about their daughter. That they had been ecstatic when they brought her home as an infant did not mean they both approved of her adult lifestyle. Father and daughter may well have had a rocky relationship. I wondered if it could have been bad enough to provoke murder.

I grabbed the envelope with D.D.'s short story and took it to the family room, where I sat with Eddie on my shoulder as I pulled the pages out of the envelope and started through the text. The hate list included no parents or sister; neither did the love list. I looked at the lists more carefully, trying to find a Teddy or a Harlow Sugar on them. The boyfriend she talked about murdering, but didn't, was named Todd. A play on Teddy? I didn't want to attribute too much to what was supposed to be fiction but it was certainly tempting.

I wanted to call Joseph and tell her my brand-new information but it was after five now and the nuns would be at evening prayers.

Eddie started crying again.

"You're a noisy one today, aren't you?" I said, standing up. "You get used to all that attention this afternoon?"

It didn't appear that he was listening to me, so I took him upstairs and got him ready for his bath.

When I'd finished eating I called Kevin Angstrom.

"Who?" he said, when I gave him my name.

"Jack Brooks's wife. We were at the Golds' on New Year's."

"Yes, sorry. My life's been one upheaval after another since that day. I know who you are. Did you know Susan's come back?"

"I heard and I'm very glad. Have you seen her?"

"Not yet. Arnold Gold doesn't want her talking to anyone. She had to beg him to let her go to work."

"Kevin, I've learned a number of things about the dead woman in the last couple of days. There was a connection between her and Susan, and I think there may have been a connection between her and you."

"Believe me, I never met the woman, I never heard of the woman."

"Bear with me, OK? I didn't mean you and she were friends. I just think there may have been something in common between you. Do you remember how you met Susan?"

"Yes. It was at an art gallery in New York, downtown, the SoHo area. Not a fancy place, just a loft where they do this kind of thing once in a while."

"Whose paintings were on exhibit?" I asked, almost holding my breath.

"They weren't paintings. They were photographs. They were done by a young Chinese woman who got them out of China. They were very interesting."

I let my breath out. That description didn't tally with anyone I knew. "Why were you there?"

"Uh, I'm not sure. I didn't know the photographer. I probably got a couple of tickets from the gallery. I'm on their mailing list."

"Do you know why Susan was there?"

"She'd heard about the photographer. In fact, I think her magazine may have been interested in doing a piece on her."

"I see."

"Have I helped you?"

"To be honest, no," I admitted. "Does that gallery send you tickets very often?"

"No, they don't. They usually just send a flyer. That may have been the only time they actually sent tickets."

"I wonder why," I said, not expecting an answer. "How long ago was that?"

"Last year sometime. I don't remember the exact date."

I tried the only name I thought might work. "Do you know an artist named Teddy Toledo?"

"Teddy, yeah. I've met him. He had a show at that gallery, I don't remember when, but it was before the one where I met Susan."

Pay dirt. "Were you friends? Have dinner together? Talk?"

"We talked. We may have had a drink at a place near the gallery once. We weren't what you would call friends."

"Kevin, Teddy knew D.D. Butler, the woman who was murdered in that farmhouse."

There was silence.

"He found the farmhouse for her. He lives up there himself, in a nearby town. He used to live in New York."

"I'm astounded. He was just a guy."

"Did you meet a woman with him?"

"It's possible. You get a crowd in those places, you can be introduced to a lot of people."

"Susan thought D.D. might have been involved in her life. I think what you've just told me indicates she was right."

"But why?"

"I don't know. Maybe it gave her some perverse pleasure to see people dance when she pulled the strings."

"But Susan and I have a real relationship."

"I know. There was nothing D.D. could do to make you fall in love—except put you together."

"Maybe Teddy killed her," he said.

"That's also possible. Kevin, I'm still trying to find my way through this. Can you tell me where Susan's father works?"

"Yes, he's an insurance broker, been one all his working life. His office is in an old building on Maiden Lane." He gave the address and the number of the office. "I've been there a couple of times. If you're a history buff, you feel like you're stepping into the past. I think his wife suggested he move uptown but he's not a person who changes easily. He likes it there and it's easy to get to from Brooklyn."

"Thanks, Kevin. I'll let you know if I learn anything more."

Then I called Jill Brady.

"You know Susan's back," she said.

"I heard. Has she been to work?"

"She came back, yes. She looks awful but she said she really wanted to work. And we're glad to have her. We're a small group and when one person is out, it hurts us all."

"Do you have your car?"

"Yes, finally. The police took it to check for prints and

blood and I don't know what else. They kept it for days but they finally gave it back to me. I gather they took it all apart."

"I wonder if they found anything," I said.

"If they did, they didn't tell me."

"Jill, were you and Susan hired about the same time?"

"We must have been. We started the same day."

"How did you get your job?"

"I was working as an assistant to an editor at a big publishing house, and he got fired and they gave me a lot of menial things to do. So I started checking the ads in the *Times* and calling friends who had jobs at other places and I found this one advertised. So I wrote a letter and sent a résumé and got an interview and they hired me."

"Just like that?" I said, impressed.

"It really was just like that. They called me to come back for a second interview, and when I walked in Jerry said I'd been hired. I can tell you I was very happy. I work harder here, but I get to do more things and that's what I wanted. If I were writing my résumé today, it would be full of the kinds of experience that appeal to people in magazine publishing. And the atmosphere here is great, very upbeat, nice people." She spoke with spirit and sincerity.

"It sounds wonderful. Do you know if Susan got her job the same way you did?"

"You know, I think she didn't. I think she once told me there was something weird about how she got the interview."

"Do you remember what she said?"

"It was like they called *her* for an interview."

"Why would they do that?"

"It was something like someone at her old job suggesting they interview her, or someone sending her résumé. I can't remember exactly but she said they came to her; she didn't go to them. But she got the job because of what she could do. It wasn't that anyone pulled strings or anything." She seemed at pains to make sure I understood Susan hadn't been hired because an arm had been twisted.

"That is weird," I agreed.

"Can I ask why you're interested in this?"

"I think it may have to do with the murder upstate."

"How?"

"I'm not sure at the moment, but these little bits of information are starting to make a pattern. When it all comes together, I'll let you know about it."

"I hope it happens soon. For Susan's sake."

I hoped so, too.

By the time Jack came home with his exciting news, I had pretty much figured it out for myself.

"Got a couple of things," he said. "The autopsy and the DNA. The DNA's very interesting."

"D.D.'s?"

"And Susan's. When Susan turned up alive, they really didn't need to continue, but it had been set in motion and the lab guy called me today. He can't prove this, but there are some important similarities between Susan's and D.D.'s DNA. He's speculating on this, but he thinks they could almost be—"

"Sisters," I said.

He looked at me. "They call here?"

"No one called. I sat and thought this evening and it came to me. Joseph, who sends you her best, by the way, said to look back at my notes from my meeting with the Donaldsons and to think about what they said. Mrs. Donaldson thought Susan was the person who rented the farmhouse. Fred didn't think so and she pooh-poohed his inability to look beyond a hairstyle. But it was more than how they combed their hair. They looked quite similar, as though they might be sisters. And then I found something that Teddy Toledo said. He's an artist, so he looks at people in a special way. He said there were superficial similarities in the looks of the two women, but they were obviously different people. That's two separate individuals who thought there was a resemblance between the two women."

"Very nice. The lab guy made a big thing about saying that DNA was most useful in exclusion rather than inclusion, and that to prove his hunch, he'd need the DNA not just from the two potential half siblings but from the three parents involved, the one they share and the two they didn't. But if he's right, you know what this means, don't you?"

"It means that something D.D. Butler's sister, Heather Williams, told me this afternoon isn't true. D.D. was adopted and she told Heather she wasn't interested in finding her birth mother. Whether Heather lied to me or D.D. lied to Heather doesn't really matter. D.D. did find her birth mother and it must be Ada Stark. And D.D. must have been doing to Ada what she was doing to Susan, insinuating herself into Ada's life and making her miserable."

"Blackmail?" Jack asked.

"Why not? Maybe she wanted from Ada everything that Susan got. She may have felt she had it coming. She was as much Ada's child as Susan was."

"What did Ada say she was doing the day of New Year's Eve?"

I tried to remember. The question had come up, I was sure of it. "I think she said she was shopping that day."

"With the family car?"

"That's my recollection. Now tell me about the autopsy."

"It's taken a long time because they had to thaw the body. What's most interesting is that they can't give a time of death. It could have been New Year's Eve, it could have been a week earlier. For that matter, it could have been a month earlier. The upstate coroner said the body would have started to cool immediately, even with wood burning in the stove, and with the kind of temperatures they've been having in that area, it would probably have frozen in twelve to twenty-four hours and only minimal changes would have taken place."

"That means we have to rely on Teddy Toledo for a last date that D.D. was alive. And that was the day before New Year's Eve."

"And you found her on January third when she was frozen solid. A three-day window."

"Which doesn't change my belief that it happened New Year's Eve."

"Or mine. The other thing that came out of the autopsy is that there was evidence of wood and ash in some of her wounds. Sounds like the killer grabbed the shovel she used to clean out the stove."

"Meaning," I said, "that he may not have gone there to kill her."

"I'm sure his lawyer'll argue that if we ever get him to court. OK. Let's talk about where we go from here."

21

If I could get in, seeing Ernest Stark seemed like a good next step. I assumed he knew nothing about what I now felt sure was the truth about Ada. Very possibly she had kept a secret, an illegitimate baby born before she married her husband, probably before she knew him. But if Ada had been sending money to D.D., Ernest might well have had suspicions of something amiss, although Ada had mentioned that she worked, and what she did with her income could well have been her own business.

But maybe he knew something about the whereabouts of his wife and daughter on New Year's Eve, and in any event, he was one of the two people I had not seen or spoken to, the other being D.D.'s adoptive father.

I couldn't call to make an appointment with Ernest Stark because I knew he wouldn't see me. My only chance was to walk in unannounced and hope he wouldn't throw me out. With no guarantee that he would even be in his office, I dropped Eddie off at Elsie's before nine on Wednesday morning and drove into the city.

Maiden Lane is in the southernmost part of Manhattan, south of the Brooklyn Bridge in what's often called the Financial District. It's a few blocks north of Wall Street and there are many old banks in the area whose reputations are solid as the structure of their buildings. Jack, who knows Manhattan better than anyone else I have ever known, described the kinds of businesses that were down there. At one time it was home to insurance companies and brokers, and many are still there.

This is the oldest part of Manhattan, where streets tend to be narrow—and one-way—with tall buildings that keep out the sun. Finding a place to leave my car wasn't easy. Uptown, the newer buildings all have basement garages. Many of these buildings were erected before cars became the preferred mode of transportation, and no thought was given as to how to get them off the street when their occupants needed to move on foot. The area is tight, so no space goes unused. There are little plazas between the buildings, and when an old building comes down, the chain-link fences go up. PARK EASY said the sign. I did, then walked back to Ernest Stark's building and looked him up in the framed directory near the elevators.

Kevin had been right about a sense of history. The floor was marble, the ceilings high, the elevators gilded cages with polished brass plates, knobs, and scrolls. I rode up to the seventh floor and walked down a long hall to Ernest Stark's office.

"May I help you?" a pleasant, graying woman at the reception desk asked.

"I'd like to see Mr. Stark."

"Do you have an appointment?"

I breathed a sigh of relief. He's in, I thought. I just have to get through the door. "No. I just found myself with a little extra time and I need to talk to him."

"Your name?"

"Ms. Bennett." I was pretty sure I had been introduced to Ada as Jack's wife, which would make me Brooks.

"Let me check." She got up and went into an office, leaving the door ajar. When she came back, she smiled. "He'll see you now."

The furnishings must have been as old as the business, a heavy desk of beautifully polished wood, an Oriental rug with plenty of wear, several wooden chairs with leather seats, shelves and books and file cabinets, and one large window looking out on nothing.

Ernest Stark was standing in the middle of the room and he held out his hand as I walked in.

"Ms. Bennett, glad to meet you. Please take a seat. What can I do for you?"

He was closer to seventy than his wife, a little thick around the waist, his hair mostly gone and what was left a thin gray. He had a warm smile, and I had the feeling he was probably a very good salesman without being pushy.

"I came here to ask you some questions, Mr. Stark. I was at the Golds' on New Year's Eve when Susan disappeared."

"You shouldn't be here, you know," he said in a fatherly way.

"I know, but I'm trying to clear Susan."

"Susan is completely innocent, and I believe she will never be charged because there isn't any evidence."

"She was there."

"I can't discuss it."

"Where were you that day, Mr. Stark?" Since he hadn't stood and ushered me out, I decided to push ahead until he did so.

"Where was I? What difference could that make?"

"It might make a difference."

"I was right here," he said, "right in this office, working, clearing out some old cases."

"How did you get here?"

"How did I travel? I think I took the subway that day."

"You own a car, don't you?"

"We do, but I take the subway when my wife needs it."

"Was anyone else here in the office that day?"

He didn't answer. He saw where I was going and he didn't want to play into my hands. Finally he said, "I don't think anyone else was in that day. Does that make a difference? Do you want to check my outgoing phone calls with the telephone company? Maybe you'll find out that someone used this phone to call my home number."

And maybe I could find out that no one had. "Do you often work here alone?"

"When I have a lot to do. I come in on the weekends sometimes. It's not something I schedule."

"Where was your wife that day?"

"I think she was out shopping. She had the day off and she wanted to visit some stores."

"Where were you when you found out Susan was missing?"

"I was here. My wife called. I went right home."

"Mr. Stark, did you see Susan in your house that morning, the morning of New Year's Eve?"

He looked beyond me. "I don't think I saw her. Was she in my house that morning?"

"I thought she was."

"I'm not sure. I'll have to ask her. I left for the office rather early."

"Did Susan ever mention the farmhouse in Bladesville where D.D. Butler's body was found?"

"Never. The first I ever heard of it was when you went up there and found the body."

"Your daughter knew her."

"I wouldn't say Susan knew that woman. And anyway, my daughter knows many people that I don't know."

I wasn't getting anywhere, and I was about to say good-bye when I thought of something else. "Before this magazine job that Susan has, where did she work?"

"For a different magazine. One of the big names."

"How did she get that job?"

"I got it for her."

His candidness startled me. "Really," I said.

"One of the fellows I went to school with owned the magazine. I called him up when Susan got out of college and asked him if he might have a job for my daughter. He said to send her down and he hired her."

"That was good luck, your knowing someone in that position."

"It was good luck, but it lasted only as long as she performed."

"I wonder why she left," I said.

"My friend retired," Ernest Stark said. "After the new management took over, there were cutbacks and downsizing and the quality of her assignments went down. When this new job came up, she took it. I think she's been very happy there."

"Do you know how she found this job?"

He shrugged. "How does anyone find any job? An ad in the paper, a lead from a friend."

I could see I had exhausted my source. I thanked him for his time and left the office.

I had to be back at Elsie's by two, a little before two to be on the safe side. Which left me quite a bit of time. Just on the chance that Ada might be home, I called her from a pay phone. She had said she worked part-time, and with luck this would be the other part. It was. She answered. I told her who it was and asked if I could come over.

"Arnold doesn't want us talking," she said.

"Ada, I'm trying to clear your daughter."

"The police will do it. Arnold will do it. I can't talk to you, Chris."

"Ada, I know the relationship between you and D.D. Butler."

There was silence. Then a voice said in a half whisper, "I'll wait here for you."

I was lucky. There was little traffic and the distance was not great. I was at her house in less than half an hour.

Her skin looked almost gray as she opened the door, her natural vitality gone, her nerves taking over. "Come in. We'll sit in the kitchen."

I took my coat off as we walked to the back of the house. She wasn't going to offer to take it. She wanted me out of there as soon as possible.

"Who knows about this?" she said as I sat at the kitchen table.

"Jack and I. The DNA looked as though Susan and D.D. Butler might be related. And I know D.D. was adopted."

Her eyes filled. Thirty-plus years of keeping a secret was withering away before her. "You talked to my husband," she said.

"He told me nothing."

"He knows nothing. How dare you do this? Didn't Arnold tell you to stay out of this?"

"Ada, your daughter may be charged with a murder. I don't think she did it." I realized as I said it that I believed it. "I think someone else did it. When did D.D. get in touch with you?"

Her mouth quivered. "A few years ago."

"How did she contact you?"

"She wrote a letter." Her voice was strained.

"What did she want?"

"To meet me. It's what they all want. Everyone's looking for roots. I was looking for a clean slate. I gave her up and I asked that the records be sealed. I didn't want to be confronted at her whim."

"Do you know how she found you?"

"She worked for an insurance company and she had a

friend who had access to records. At least that's what she told me."

"What did she want?"

"The world. Everything she'd been denied when I gave her up."

"Were you paying her?"

She nodded, nearly in tears.

"Was she threatening you?"

"She said she would tell Ernie if I didn't pay her. He doesn't know. Ernie has never known anything about it. It was my choice when I met him and I've never changed my mind. I didn't want him to know." She paused. "I still don't."

"Did you ever meet D.D.?"

"Never. I didn't want to and I told her that. She wasn't part of my life. There's a lot more to being a mother than giving birth. Even if I had adopted Susan, she would be my daughter when D.D. wasn't. I've shared Susan's life. That's what makes me her mother."

"What about D.D.'s natural father?"

"There was never any question of our getting married. He was a wealthy man, older than I, married with a couple of children. I was young and inexperienced and very taken with him. I was quite pretty when I was young," she added, as though to explain his interest in her.

"I'm sure you were, Ada. You're a very beautiful woman."

Two tears spilled over. "Thank you," she said softly.

"So you gave birth even though you knew you would give the baby away."

"It was over thirty years ago. Abortions were illegal and often dangerous. He would have paid for one. He would have preferred that I have one. Maybe that's why I didn't. And maybe I held out some hope that when our child was born—" She stopped as the pain became too much.

He would see their beautiful child and he would leave his wife. He would do the honorable thing. Nine months of hopes and fears, and in the end the inevitable happened.

"Did you ever see him again?"

"Never."

"Is his name on D.D.'s birth certificate?"

"No."

"Ada, Susan spent the night before New Year's Eve in this house."

"How do you know that?"

"She told me."

"She what?"

"We spoke," I said.

"But Arnold said she wasn't—"

"I know, but she wants me to help her clear her name."

"My God."

"I think she knew about you and D.D." As I said it, I realized Susan had a good motive for killing her half sister, to protect their mother. If Susan knew that D.D. was blackmailing Ada . . .

"How could she—?"

"If a letter came to the house, she could have found it and read it."

"I thought I was so careful."

"Ada, do you have any papers in the house about D.D.?"

"Not anymore. I used to have a birth certificate years ago. Ernie never goes near anything of mine and I thought it was perfectly safe. Later on, when Susan was growing up, I got rid of it."

"Did it have D.D.'s name on it?"

"It just said Baby Girl."

Funny how puzzling bits and pieces start to make

sense. "You know, when Susan was a child she thought she was adopted."

"Many children think that," Ada said. "It's not uncommon."

"But her fear persisted. She told people about it."

"She must have seen the papers and misunderstood them." She looked even sadder. "It's hard to imagine Susan rummaging around in my things."

"She was a child. Little girls are very curious."

"And big girls, it appears, if she read the letters D.D. sent."

It seemed an ironic twist on the usual. Here it wasn't the inquisitive mother snooping through her daughter's possessions; it was the curious child, the suspicious young adult, reading her mother's mail, copying down a name and address. Perhaps the suspicious adult had grown directly from the child who had accidentally found something in Mommy's drawer while innocently searching for a Band-Aid or a favorite piece of jewelry.

"On New Year's Eve," I said, changing the subject, "when did you find out that Susan was missing?"

"Kevin called to talk to her. You've heard all this before."

"I know. Tell me again."

"He said he'd dropped her off here the afternoon before, and I hadn't seen her. He was worried and that made me worried."

"What did you do?"

She thought for a moment, as thought there might be a part of the story she had to remember. "I called Ernie."

"Where?"

"At his office."

"Was he there?"

"Of course, he was there. I told him what had happened and he came right home."

They all covered for each other. "Where were you that day, Ada?"

"I had the day off. I took the car and went shopping."

"Where?"

"Here and there." She seemed nervous but the whole situation was so tense, it was hard to draw any conclusions from it.

"Where is here and where is there?" I asked pointedly.

"I went—I drove to New Jersey. I like to shop there. There's no sales tax and there are wonderful outlets."

"Did you buy anything?"

"Just a few little—" Her voice faded.

"Little whats? What did you buy, Ada?"

"A pair of shoes, I think."

"Did you charge them?"

"Is this an inquisition? Do I have to prove what I paid?"

"I am trying to find out where you were that day," I said. "I want to know whether you were really shopping or whether you drove upstate to Bladesville and killed D.D. Butler, who was blackmailing you."

"Get out," she said. "Go away. I can't talk anymore. I can't think anymore." Her voice broke. "Please go away."

I looked at my watch. I had a baby to feed and a long drive to get to him. I stood and buttoned my coat. Then I patted Ada's shoulder. "I'm sorry," I said. It was an understatement.

22

Late that evening, before Jack came home but long after I had put Eddie to sleep, I dialed Ernest Stark's business number. It rang several times and then an answering machine picked up, telling me what the office hours were and inviting me to leave a message. I didn't. The message I had gotten was that if Ada had called her husband on New Year's Eve to tell him that their daughter was missing, the machine could just as easily have picked up and a completed call from the Starks' residence to the Starks' business would show on telephone company records, proving nothing. Maybe Ernest Stark was there and maybe he wasn't. Maybe he knew his wife's whereabouts that day and was covering for her. Maybe one or both of the Starks knew that Susan was home the night before New Year's Eve and maybe they didn't.

The plain fact was that either of the Stark women could have driven up to Bladesville and killed D.D. And since we knew that Susan had gone, what was equally plain was that her mother could have gone, too. Ernest might have been home and might know when Ada left and returned.

Or perhaps I had to come full circle and look at Susan a little harder. By her own admission, Susan had gone to the farmhouse. It was perfectly possible that Ada had spent the day shopping in New Jersey and Ernie had spent the day working alone in his office. For a short time I had convinced myself of Susan's innocence. The simplest explanation was that she had killed D.D. and removed all traces of identification and all indications that there was a connection to her mother. During the days of her disappearance she could have burned or otherwise destroyed the evidence. There were no computers involved here. The most sophisticated piece of equipment in the farmhouse was a manual typewriter. If you went through the house and removed all the paper, you had everything. Maybe it was as simple as it looked.

I turned it all over and over, looking at how each of the Starks covered for the others, how each could be telling the truth or just as easily could be lying. But there was more to the story than the murder. There was D.D.'s project, her play, her scenario if you like. This was not merely a story of blackmail and revenge. It was not simply that one or two of the Starks had decided to end D.D.'s life on New Year's Eve. D.D. was expecting them—or someone—that day. It was even possible that what had happened to her was what she had plotted for her killer in a scheme that had gone awry. She could have planned to invite one of these people to come up, kill the visitor, and leave the house in the visitor's car. Then everything would have happened in reverse. D.D. would have cleared out her things from the house and left the victim's body to be discovered in the spring. Her rent was paid up for another month, so no one was likely to come by for more money. She could call Teddy Toledo and tell him she'd left so he wouldn't come to take her shopping, and she could write a letter to the Donaldsons saying that she had left, thank you very much. Or even, I thought, send a check for another month or two to keep the Donaldsons from going to the house and discovering the body.

The question I had to answer had now become: Who had D.D. invited to her murderous New Year's Eve party? For sure, Susan had been invited. And who else?

I got the envelope with D.D.'s short story and looked again at the lists of people she loved and people she hated. Was this the key? Or was I overreacting, taking a piece of fiction and translating it into real murderous intent?

I read the whole story through from start to finish. Except for the lists, there didn't seem to be much else that was helpful. Todd, the boyfriend (Teddy? I wondered again), narrowly escaped the narrator's wrath. The poor victim, whose death came in the last paragraph, was a stranger who didn't seem to have committed any injustice against the narrator, but he was handy. Far from luring him to her home, she met him in a park at night, possibly Central Park from the description, where she killed him on a park bench and walked away. It was a gruesome story and I wondered more than once why it had been published.

If anything were a clue to D.D.'s troubled psyche, it had to be the lists. Number one on the hate list: the Big Boss. God? The person she worked for at the insurance company? Second was the Little Boss. Then there were a number of apparent abbreviations, none of which meant anything to me. The love list was just as opaque. With a little blurring of letters, one name on it took on a familiar look: Weather Girl was pretty close to Heather W.

Eventually, the whole thing blurred and I fell asleep.

"It's a nice theory," Jack said. He had eaten and I had nursed Eddie, and we were getting ready for bed. "D.D. invites the people she's most angry at or jealous of: her natural mother who gave her up and doesn't send her enough money and her half sister who lives what she thinks is the better life. She's going to kill one or both of them and drive off. What's she going to do with the second car?"

"There are plenty of buildings on that farm. There's a barn that could hold several cars. She could stash one car there and take the other one. Maybe she had a ticket to leave the country."

"Let me think about this a minute," Jack said, and I knew I had his full interest. "We've ruled out Ernest because if he knew he'd take Ada in his arms and say, 'I don't give a damn,' and tell her to stop paying. Or he'd say, 'I've found you out and it's all over between us.'"

"Sounds right to me."

"So maybe Ada went up and found Susan after she committed the murder. Or didn't find Susan but found D.D.'s body. She comes back to Brooklyn, and after Kevin calls to ask for Susan, who is now missing, possibly because her mother told her to get lost for a while, Ada calls Ernie's number so that there'll be a record of the call, making it appear that she has just learned of Susan's disappearance."

"I can buy that. Are we back to suspecting Susan?"

"I don't know. A couple of things are tickling my mind."

"Uh-oh," I said. I smiled and looked at myself sideways in the mirror over my dresser.

"You look good."

"There's still a bump where my flat stomach used to be."

"Suck it in, babe. The way New York's Finest do when photographers show up."

I laughed. "Joseph said there were so many magazines in this case. Susan worked for one. D.D. was published in more than one. I think I'll call Harlow Sugar in the morning. I want to find out who published this terrible story of D.D.'s. And something else. If you run into a boring day, could you check and see if there are any unsolved murders in Central Park? A body left on a bench?"

"There are bound to be. Most homicides go unsolved, you know. Excepting those my wife has a hand in solving. What makes you think there's a connection?"

"I forced myself to read that awful story through from start to finish tonight. The first time, I skimmed it except for the lists. This time I read it carefully. The narrator kills someone on a park bench. The last sentence was, 'Practice makes perfect.' "

"Wow."

"My very thought."

I called Harlow Sugar the next morning. There was no answer. I didn't know whether he worked at home or in an office, how much time he spent in either, or exactly where I was calling, but I assumed it was his home since I had found the number in the phone book under his name. Perhaps he would be back later.

It was a little milder this morning and I took Eddie out for a walk, pointing out Mel's house as we passed it. I missed Mel a lot. We had become friends when I moved into Aunt Meg's house after leaving St. Stephen's, and I had learned to count on her friendship and her proximity. Through Mel I had found a place in the community for myself, council meetings to attend, issues to be concerned about on election day. There had been wonderful afternoons filled with tea and cookies and conversation, and on occasion I had baby-sat for her so she and Hal could go out with a sense of security.

Now she was working and I was tied to a schedule of

feeding my baby every four hours. The fluidity and changeability of life had never before been so apparent.

"Nothing is static," I said to my sleeping son. "Look at you, gaining an ounce a day while I try to lose twice that."

A car slowed and my next-door neighbor, Midge MacDonald, rolled down the window and called hello.

"Hi," I called back.

"Nice day, huh?"

"Beautiful."

"Come around some afternoon. I like babies."

"Thanks, I will." We waved and she drove on down the street.

I turned around and went back, hoping to reach Harlow Sugar before lunch.

"Hello," his voice sounded.

"Mr. Sugar, I'm glad I found you. It's Chris Bennett."

"Chris Bennett."

"I talked to you about D.D. Butler."

"Right. I remember. Did you get that piece I sent you?"

"Got it, and I thank you very much."

"Not exactly bedtime reading."

"No, it's pretty gloomy. I wanted to ask you about the magazine it was published in. Do you have the name?"

"Sure. I have the whole thing. I just Xeroxed those pages and sent them to you."

"Can you give me the name, address, whatever else is there?"

"Hang on." He went away, humming some strange tune that I heard for the whole time he was searching for the magazine. "OK. Got it. What do you want to know?"

"The name, to begin with."

"*Soupçon*—I'm not sure how to pronounce it." He read off the Manhattan address.

"Any phone number?"

"Yeah." He gave that to me, too.

"What does the magazine look like?" I asked. "Kind of amateurish?"

"Amateurish, hell no. It's a good-looking glossy."

"I'm surprised," I admitted. "I didn't think the quality of that story was very good and it's hard to believe it had wide appeal."

"Appeal or not, it's a very professional-looking job."

"What's the name of the publisher or editor-in-chief?"

"The name at the top here is Melissa Hanes. You planning on calling her?"

"I may."

"Can I ask why?"

"I'm curious about a story like D.D.'s appearing in what sounds like a mainstream magazine. Did you read any of the other stories?"

"To be completely truthful I didn't. I knew D.D. and when the story came out, I got myself one copy. But I looked through the rest of it. There's a French story here in translation, a story by a gal I've heard of," he gave me a familiar name, "a bunch of poems—I don't read poetry so I can't comment."

"That's very interesting. Thank you very much, Mr. Sugar."

"Hey, glad to be of service."

I called the number he had given me for *Soupçon* and asked for Melissa Hanes. I had to identify myself and they passed me off to a young assistant. "I'd like to talk to Ms. Hanes," I said.

A perky voice said, "She's busy now. Can I help you?"

"I have a question about someone you published last year, D.D. Butler."

"I remember that name. What can I tell you?"

I felt very frustrated. I wanted to get into a conversation with Melissa Hanes, not with her young assistant. "Is D.D. a personal friend of Ms. Hanes?"

"I'm sure I wouldn't know. Can I ask why you want to know that?"

"D.D. died recently and—"

"Oh," she said, with shock. "I'm sorry to hear it."

"It's just that I thought she might be Melissa Hanes's friend and if I could talk to her—" I let it hang, hoping she would bite.

"Let me see if she can talk to you now."

Obviously, Melissa Hanes's calendar was less full than I had been led to believe. She picked up in seconds.

"This is Melissa Hanes. Who is this, please?"

"I'm Chris Bennett. I have some questions about D.D. Butler."

"D.D. Butler, yes. We published a story of hers a few issues ago."

"That's the one. I thought the story was a little unusual for your magazine."

"We publish a variety of fiction. May I ask what your interest is in this?"

"D.D. Butler died about two weeks ago."

"Oh," she said. Then, "I hadn't heard."

"Did you know her?"

"Not really. I never met her. She sent the story to me and I may have spoken to her once or twice on the phone after that. She was paid for that story and we've had no contact with her since. What is the point of this?"

"It appears that D.D. was murdered," I said, "and there are some loose ends I'm trying to tie up. Can you tell me how you decided to publish her story? Was it your decision or do you have an editorial board that makes that decision?" I really didn't think they had a huge staff. However beautiful the magazine might look, there couldn't be an awful lot of money in it.

"That story—you know, that's not an easy question to answer."

"In general or for that story?"

"Our usual procedure is to read and review every submission. We're a small organization and we make our decisions through discussion."

"And on this story?"

"I really don't want to discuss this story. We published it and we paid for it; it's done. I don't know who you are or what your interest is. I'm sorry Ms. Butler's dead but I really can't help you any further."

She sounded angry and anxious to end the conversation so we ended it. She may have thought—or hoped— that she wasn't helpful, but the fact that D.D.'s story got published without going through the usual procedure and evoked these emotions in the editor made me feel that something was truly unusual. It hadn't been a wasted phone call.

Jack called in the afternoon while Eddie and I were having a kind of conversation.

"I looked up your possible Central Park–unsolved-park-bench homicide and there wasn't any."

"It was just a thought."

"But I found one somewhere else. Tompkins Square Park."

"Tompkins Square. Over on the Lower East Side, right?"

"Right. The precinct cops call it Alphabet City."

"Jack, that's not too far from where D.D.'s last apartment was."

"That's just what I was thinking. The case is still

marked open and the squad is still putting in D.D.5s periodically, but no heavy work is being done."

"When did it happen?"

"About a year ago. How does that fit with your theory?"

"It fits. She was still living in New York. Her story was published around that time. Do you know who the victim was?"

"A homeless guy. According to the file he was known in the area as Curly. That ring a bell?"

It didn't, but I told him I would see if I could make anything of it. When I got off the phone I went back to the lists in the story. There was no one like Curly on either one. The victim was Lester Heim and his looks were never described. I ran my eyes up and down the two lists, returning to poor Lester's name until something finally clicked.

"Come on, Eddie. Let's take a little ride in the car." I scooped him up, changed him, and dressed him for the outdoors. Then I drove us to the library.

Oakwood has quite a good library, and the reference desk sent me to the foreign dictionaries right away. I was carrying Eddie in a pouch on my chest, leaving my arms free. I tried the German dictionary first. *Heim* was a German word and it translated to "home." Lester Home. Les Home. Maybe it was my overactive imagination, but by reversing the two names you could come up with an understandable version of "homeless." Whether D.D. had written the story before or after the murder, as far as I was concerned, she had pretty much confessed to it in print.

23

When we came home I called Susan's father and was put through with no difficulty.

"I'm talking to you," he said, "but I have nothing to say."

"I have one question. What was the name of the man who gave Susan her first job?"

"That's easy. It was Irwin Liebowitz. Irv and I grew up together before his father got rich. When their circumstances changed, the family moved to a big apartment on the East Side of Manhattan but we stayed friends. Eventually, Irv took over his father's job. His son didn't want it and Irv sold to a conglomerate a couple of years ago."

"How many magazines do they publish?"

"I never counted. I would say just the right amount. They provided well for the family and didn't work either Irv or his father into a premature grave. His father lived to be almost ninety."

I appreciated the commentary. I thanked him and called Jack to tell him what I'd learned in the library.

"That's a neat piece of deduction," Jack said. "Any chance it's a coincidence?"

"Sure, there's a chance. But the narrator calls him Les several times in the story. I checked. It's as if D.D. wanted to be found out."

"Well, I'll call the detective in charge of the Curly

homicide and see what he thinks. From what you've said, all she was doing was practicing for the big killing on New Year's Eve."

"That's just what I think. D.D. had a grudge against her birth mother for giving her up and then not being willing to accept her as a family member, and maybe she had a bigger grudge against Susan for being the beneficiary of everything D.D. wanted for herself. So she steered Susan into Kevin's arms and into a good job just so she could take it all away."

"Then you think Susan was the target on New Year's Eve?"

"I do. By killing Susan, D.D. could ruin Ada's life."

"Sounds like D.D. was already over the deep end a long time before New Year's Eve."

"She had to be," I agreed. "Sane, normal people don't plan murders and don't commit practice ones."

"This is some story," Jack said. "It looks like we're back to suspecting Susan."

"Or Ada or Ernie. But there are loose ends I'm trying to figure out. There's something very strange about that story of D.D.'s. We'll talk about it tonight. I don't want to keep you from your real work."

He made an appropriate comment and we hung up. Loose ends. I wondered if they mattered. Would finding out more about how D.D.'s story got published help me to determine which of the Starks had killed her?

The person I really wanted to talk to was Arnold. We hadn't exchanged a word since Susan came back and he asked me to get off the case. I wondered whether he knew as much as I did about the life and times of D.D. Butler. I was sure Jack and I were the only two living people who suspected she had murdered the homeless man in Tompkins Square Park. Whether that could ever be proven was still doubtful. There was no chance for a confession if you didn't consider the short story to be that. I picked up the phone.

"Chris, it's a tough life," Arnold answered. "How are you?"

"I'm fine."

"And our beautiful baby? Harriet asks me every day when she can talk to you again. I'm sorry this has happened."

"Eddie's wonderful, almost two months old. We'll be going back to the pediatrician next week for his checkup."

"Well, that sounds good. I'm glad you're all well. I've missed talking to you, as you can imagine. I understand my client defied my judgment and went to see you."

"She did. She told me a few things I didn't know but she left gaping holes in her story. I told her I wouldn't look into the case till she filled in the blanks."

"But you kept looking anyway."

I smiled. Arnold knew me well. "There were things that were crying out to be uncovered."

"And you answered the cry. I've gotten some info from the Bladesville sheriff's department that I gather comes originally from you. They the same folks who didn't want you nursing your baby outside a concrete fortress?"

"The very same." It was such a pleasure to be talking to him again I hardly cared what the subject was. "I've learned some things you may want to know, Arnold."

"About this Toledo character?"

"You've probably heard all there is to know about him."

"You think he's a suspect?"

"A long shot. He had opportunity, but I can't see what he would have gained. Are you aware that D.D. Butler was responsible for Susan and Kevin meeting?"

"Tell me more."

I did, continuing on to the peculiar way Susan got her second job.

"I don't know what's significant anymore. It's one of my loose ends. Arnold, I've found the secrets that Susan kept from me."

"I figured you would. It's why I didn't want you to keep digging. What direction does that point you?"

"I think one, two, or all three of the Starks had a hand in the murder."

"Well, you can't expect me to comment on that."

"I think some or all of them were lured there by D.D. Butler. I believe she wanted to kill them and they turned the tables on her."

"It looks as though she was hit with something like a shovel, not an easy or pleasant way to commit that kind of crime. I don't think my client is capable of it."

"I also think D.D. herself had already killed before New Year's Eve." I went on to tell him what Jack and I had just discussed.

"That's a hell of a discovery," Arnold said. "Want to give me the magazine and anything else you've got?"

I read it off to him, explaining my theories about the names on the lists. It was clearly all new to him and every piece of information was important. When he had it all down, I asked if he had spoken to anyone in the Butler family.

"They've all been questioned. Seem like nice enough people who can't quite believe what's happened. If you want to know whether one of them could have killed D.D. Butler, they'd have to have been in two places at the same time."

"Including the father?"

"Most especially the father. He worked on New Year's Eve and the day before that. A lot of people saw him."

"Well, that's about all I can tell you. If anything else comes up, I'll give you a call. Give Harriet a kiss for me."

"I will. And I'm sure I can trust you to keep family secrets to yourself."

"Absolutely."

Eddie was doing his late-afternoon thing by then, feeling irritable and letting me know it. I tried talking to him but he would have none of it. I even tried singing an old children's song that I remembered from a long time ago, but I guess my voice didn't have the necessary soothing qualities. He was almost two months old and I started wondering when I should get a playpen for him. There was plenty of room in the family room and I could be in the kitchen and keep my eye on him. I would have to ask Mel. She always knew the answers to such questions.

I realized as my mind wandered that it had suddenly become quiet. Eddie was on my shoulder and he was fast asleep. Good, I thought. I had one more call to make and this was a perfect time, too early for a husband to be home. I stood carefully, supporting Eddie's head, and went to the kitchen phone, carrying him.

Ada answered on the second ring.

"It's Chris. I have a couple of questions. Was D.D. blackmailing her natural father?"

"I don't know."

"Did she know who he was?"

"Chris, you're asking me questions that are hard for me to answer."

"You said his name wasn't on her birth certificate. I assume that means you wrote 'Unknown' when you were asked."

"That's right."

"Was there any record anywhere of his name?"

"None that I know of."

"Did you tell D.D. his name?"

"Please," she said.

"Did D.D. know who he was?"

"Yes." Her voice was choked. "She asked me and I told her. She threatened me if I didn't."

"What's his name, Ada?"

"I can't—"

"Think of Susan," I said. "Do you want her charged with murder?"

I heard something that sounded like a sob. Then she said, "Bill. His name was Bill Childs."

"Do you know where he lives?"

"No."

"When did you tell her?"

"I'm not sure. A long time ago. A year or more."

"Thank you, Ada. I know how hard this has been for you."

So D.D. knew her father's name and had known it for some time. It threw a new light on things. If Ada had really kept his name a secret, then no one could have known who D.D.'s natural father was till Ada disclosed the name herself. I had to wonder now whether he had been invited to the family reunion in Bladesville on New Year's Eve.

The name Bill Childs didn't quite ring a bell, but it sounded as though I might have heard it somewhere. I pulled out the Manhattan phone book and looked it up. There was nothing. I called information and asked for a listing under that name. I was told the number for William J. Childs was not published at the request of the customer. So he lived in the city and wasn't listed. I called Jack, hoping to get him before he left for the day. On my shoulder, little Eddie seemed happy to snuggle.

"Jack, I need some help from your esteemed department," I said when I got him on the phone.

"Esteemed? You looking for a private audience with the commissioner?"

"Not quite. I need to know where a man named William J. Childs lives. He's got a Manhattan residence but no listed number."

"Who is this guy?"

"D.D. Butler's natural father."

"Who broke down and gave you his name?"

"Ada. Reluctantly. I'd guess that by now he's in his sixties anyway. He was married with children when they had their affair and that was over thirty years ago."

"Maybe he owns a car," Jack said. "I'll do what I can. I may not have time to call back."

"That's OK. I'm not going anywhere tonight."

"Kiss my son for me."

"Done."

"Brewster, New York," I said when Jack handed me a piece of paper with the name and address. "Rich and powerful."

"And not too far from here. He has two cars registered at that address. Probably has an apartment in the city for when he entertains the mayor. Where are you taking this?"

"He may be the missing piece in my puzzle. I think tomorrow I'll be able to find out."

It was another long shot situation, where I would have to pretend to know things I merely suspected were possible. A little after nine on Friday morning I called *Soupçon* and asked to speak to Melissa Hanes. This time my name worked; she came on the line immediately.

"Ms. Hanes, are you the daughter of William J. Childs?"

"I—yes, I am. How did you know?"

"It seemed logical," I said, hoping to sound vague. "Is your father the owner of *Soupçon*?"

"I am the owner," she said archly.

"Did your father ask you to publish D.D. Butler's story?"

"What business is that of yours?" she retorted, making me feel I had hit the jackpot.

"It's part of the business of D.D. Butler's life and death."

"I publish what I choose to publish."

"Did your father ask you to do it as a favor?"

"Why do you care?" she persisted. "How can this possibly have anything to do with you?"

"He did, didn't he?" I said.

"He asked me, yes. My father was always very good to me. It seemed a small thing to do."

"Was there anything else? Other stories of hers?"

"There was nothing else. He just asked if I could publish it quickly. I had to remove an article from that issue because there was no more room."

"Thank you, Ms. Hanes." I knew what I needed to. Now I had to talk to William Childs.

I called information and asked for the Brewster phone number but it was unlisted. There was no certainty that he would be at the Brewster address since he also had the apartment in New York, but if he wasn't there, perhaps a caretaker could be persuaded to give me the Manhattan address or a business address. It was worth a try.

Elsie agreed to take Eddie on short notice, and when I handed him to her I was sure I saw a glint of recognition in his face. He was awake and she greeted him like an old friend, as a little smile moved his lips.

"He's a little chunkier than last time I saw him, isn't he?" she said approvingly.

"I think so. And I'm afraid he's outgrowing all those little clothes I've been putting on him."

"Those little things don't last long, Chris. You'll be surprised how fast he goes from one size to the next. Look at you," she said, beaming at Eddie. "You are wonderful. You are just wonderful."

And on that note I left them.

Brewster is almost due north of Oakwood, just west of the Connecticut state line in New York State. I had never been there although I'd passed road signs for it for years. I was kind of nervous at the prospect of meeting William Childs. I knew things about him that he had kept secret for over thirty years, and for my personal safety I would have to make it very plain that my-husband-the-police-sergeant knew where I was and why I had come.

It was a beautiful town, the kind I could never afford to live in, but it was fun to drive through the streets. When I finally reached the Childs house, which looked more like an estate than just a house, I turned into a private road that led to the front door. I parked at the side, leaving plenty of room for other cars, and walked up to a pair of double doors with beautiful brass fittings.

The door was opened by a middle-aged woman wearing a brown dress that wasn't quite a uniform but wasn't anything else. "May I help you?"

"My name is Christine Bennett. I'd like to see Mr. Childs."

She looked over at my ancient car and then studied me for a few seconds. "What is the nature of your business, Ms. Bennett?"

"It has to do with his daughter Melissa's magazine, *Soupçon*."

"Please wait here."

"Here" was in the large foyer. I stepped in a little farther, hoping to see someone through a doorway, but the nearby rooms were empty. The woman in the brown dress had disappeared silently and I could hear no voices. It was the quietest house I had ever been in. I found myself listening for footsteps, for anything that marked a sign of life.

Finally the woman returned. She gave me a half smile. "Come this way, please."

I followed her into a room that looked more lived-in than the ones near the front of the house. There were many windows, and a lot of plants and even trees spaced around where they could soak up light. A slim, grayish-haired woman in a black dress that barely covered her knees stood waiting for me. A pin with glittering stones that I took to be diamonds adorned the plain dress and picked up sparkles of light as she moved.

"I'm Mrs. Childs," she said. "You are—"

"Christine Bennett. I'm sorry to intrude. I want to—"

"Do you live in Brewster?" she interrupted.

"I live in Oakwood."

"How did you find this address?"

"It was a stroke of luck."

"I wonder," Mrs. Childs said with obvious skepticism. "How can I help you, Ms. Bennett?"

"If I could talk to your husband . . ."

"My husband is dead, Ms. Bennett."

"I'm so sorry," I said, feeling the shock of her words.

"So I'm afraid you've driven a long way for nothing."

"When did he die?" I asked.

"In December. It's a month tomorrow. It was a heart attack, very sudden." The black dress, the stack of letters she was writing on the desk.

"I apologize for the intrusion." I hadn't sat because she

hadn't invited me to and was still standing herself. I started to turn toward the door when she spoke.

"Can I help you with something?"

"I don't think so." There was nothing I could say that would not give away her husband's secret.

The woman in brown was waiting just outside the room. I followed her to the front door.

24

"Well, that was hardly a visit," Elsie said as she saw me at the front door. "Come on in and have lunch with me before you go."

I really wanted to get home and make a phone call but I couldn't turn her down. Eddie was fast asleep in Elsie's crib, and I tiptoed out after I looked in on him and went downstairs where Elsie was enlarging an already put-together salad. "Looks great," I said.

"Well, they've got such a variety of greens nowadays and I keep hearing how good they are for you. Come sit, and you tell me what's going on in your life."

I obliged her and we had a good time eating and talking till Eddie woke up. Then I nursed him and packed us up and drove home. I knew Eddie would sleep for a little while anyway, giving me time to find out what I could about the Childs publishing empire, if that's what it was. I knew now that William Childs could not have killed D.D. Butler. Whether she was murdered on New Year's Eve or a day earlier or later, she surely hadn't been murdered thirty days ago. Today was January fifteenth. Teddy Toledo had seen her shortly before the New Year's Eve weekend.

I dug out the address of *Cool Times*, smiling at the memory of Harlow Sugar's description of Billy Luft with his shirt open to his navel and a bunch of chains adorning his naked chest.

"Billy Luft," his voice answered, and I noted how much more accessible he was than Melissa Hanes.

"Mr. Luft, it's Chris Bennett. We talked a week ago about D.D. Butler."

"Right. About her photo-essay. You find her?"

"Not exactly. Mr. Luft, who owns *Cool Times*?"

"I do. What does that have to do with D.D.?"

"Are you related to William Childs?"

The explosion of laughter forced me to pull the phone away from my ear. "You kidding?"

"I'm very serious."

"If you're serious, I'll be serious. I never met the man in my life."

"What was so funny about my question?"

"Childs is rich. Childs is what we'd all like to be sooner or later. Preferably sooner."

"Then he didn't have anything to do with your publishing D.D.'s photo-article?"

"William Childs? You've lost me. Is there something here I'm missing?"

"No. I think I'm looking in the wrong place. Tell me, how did you come to publish D.D.'s piece?"

"She showed it to me. I liked it. In this business you go with your gut. Mine is usually full of Maalox but it still functions."

"So you have no connection to William Childs."

"Not a one."

"But you've heard of him."

"Sure I've heard of him."

"I understand his daughter is Melissa Hanes."

"You bet. She publishes a magazine with an unpronounceable name."

"Soupçon," I said in my best French. "Did her father set up the magazine for her?"

"You bet he did," Billy Luft said. "He was a world-class daddy. Set the kids up the way they wanted and kept control of his empire."

There was that word. "Did he own a lot of magazines?"

"Enough. He died, didn't he?"

"About a month ago," I said. "I tried to see him and found out. That's why I'm calling you."

"Well, I can tell you I'm not in his class. Yet."

"You said he set the kids up. Were there other kids besides Melissa?"

"He had a son. Same name as his dad but I think he goes by Jerry."

"Oh my."

"Sounds like something just rang a bell."

"I think it did. Can you tell me the name of Jerry's magazine?"

"Yeah, I think I can. It's fairly new. Lemme think. How does *Single Up* sound?"

"It sounds like I just hit the jackpot." That was the name of Susan Stark's magazine.

It was Friday and Jack would be home for dinner, his law classes meeting only the first four nights of the week. I reached him at his desk and told him quickly what I had learned.

"Sounds like the son has just become your best suspect."

"I think it's worth finding him and talking to him, don't you?"

"You bet. Got his address?"

"What do you think I'm calling about?"

"Aha."

"Does that mean you'll look it up? I've got his phone

number. I called him when Susan was first missing. His number was on the answering machine message at the magazine. He's the one who told me to call Jill Brady."

"Interesting. That would mean he had no idea Susan was planning to drive up to Bladesville."

"Maybe he didn't know. I doubt whether Susan talked to him about it. Presumably she had no idea he was related to D.D."

"Exactly the way she was."

"I hadn't thought of that. They were each half siblings. Anyway, here's the number." I knew he could find the address in *Cole's* directory, where numbers are listed first. He promised to bring it home with him. There wasn't anything else I could do that afternoon anyway.

Since I am the lesser cook in the family, I tend to stick to simpler fare and let Jack jazz up our culinary life over the weekend. I had bought a nice roast beef for tonight and decided this was the time to use a Christmas present from Mel, a popover pan, for the first time. I had seasoned it as soon as I got it but hadn't had the opportunity to use it yet. Following the directions that came with the pan, I mixed the batter and chilled it till the moment Jack arrived. Then I put it in the very hot oven I had preheated, and stood in the kitchen like a kid, watching through the glass window as they rose. It was better than a movie.

"Something smells fantastic," Jack said, giving me a kiss.

"Look." I pointed to the sideshow in the oven.

"Real popovers. I haven't had them—"

"At least not since we got married. You can thank Mel. She always knows what to give me that won't tax my talents too much. I miss her so much, Jack. She's back at school and those ten great days she was off seem like a year ago."

"Well, make some time. You could visit her in the afternoon, when she gets home from school."

"I guess so." I had thought about it a lot. I thought about how tired Mel must be after teaching little kids for so many hours, and how late afternoon was when Eddie fussed. If I took him to her house, would he rattle her with his crying? And on the other hand, was I worrying too much?

Dinner turned out to be astoundingly good, thanks to those popovers. I don't know what possessed me to think I would have half of them left over but there were none. We consumed one after another, laughing at our self-indulgence.

"Hey, it's eggs and milk," Jack said at one point. "How bad can that be for you?"

I didn't bother arguing. I just enjoyed myself.

Jack had found an address for William J. Childs, Jr. He lived in Tenafly, New Jersey, an upscale suburb of New York just across the George Washington Bridge. Tomorrow was Saturday, a good time to find him home. But finding him and talking to him would not uncloak him as a murderer, if he were, indeed, the killer. We needed solid evidence, something that would prove he had been in that farmhouse and committed the murder. The autopsy was inconclusive on the time of D.D.'s death. More than two weeks after I assumed the crime had been committed, it would be hard for a person to account for where he'd been during that period. If he said he was at home, who could prove he was not?

I arranged to leave Eddie with Elsie. Since there were detectives in Brooklyn who were interested in Susan as the only suspect, and a detective in Bladesville who was presumably still looking for an elusive murderer, Jack didn't bother calling either one. If there were an arrest to be made, it would be the local police who would do it.

We drove over in the morning, getting there about eleven-thirty. The house, while quite expensive, didn't match the one the older Mrs. Childs lived in in Brewster. A three-car garage had one door up and a vacant space inside. Somebody was out.

There didn't seem to be anybody around outside the house. The walks and drive were all well cleared of snow, and it was now so long since the last heavy snowfall that concrete and blacktop were visible everywhere. Jack and I walked up to the front door and a few seconds after I rang, a woman about my age opened it. She was casually dressed, but with an elegance I doubted I would ever achieve.

"Yes?" she said with a smile.

"I'm Chris Bennett. I'm looking for Mr. Childs."

"He's out. Can I ask what this is about?"

Jack moved away, presumably because my safety wasn't in jeopardy with this young woman.

Jack and I had talked about what to do in case Mr. Childs was home, and in case Mrs. Childs was. So I was using Plan B. "I've been looking into a rather strange occurrence around New Year's Eve. A young woman who works for your husband at the magazine disappeared for several days and—"

"Come on in. It's freezing."

"Thanks." I was happy for the invitation.

We went into her house and I took my coat off and carried it. She led the way to a small room that must have been her private study, with a small desk in one corner. She took one of the comfortable chairs and offered the other to me. The walls of the room were covered with family photos. I remembered my telephone conversation with her husband and the sounds of children in the background. They were a boy and a girl, the older one probably no more than kindergarten age.

"You were saying something about someone who works for my husband."

"Susan Stark."

"Yes, he's mentioned her name. I'm sure she's not still missing. He talked about her the other day."

"She came back, but it appears she may have been involved in an unpleasant matter."

"But's it's nothing involving my husband."

"Oh, I don't think he's involved in her disappearance in any way," I reassured her, hoping to gain her confidence. "But she's said some very strange things that I'd like to clear up."

"Who are you, exactly?" she asked uneasily.

"I'm a friend of Susan's family and I've done some work for her lawyer." The first part of the statement was an exaggeration and the second part the truth, but neither had much to do with my quest for answers. "Did you and your husband go out on New Year's Eve, Mrs. Childs?"

"Yes we did. It was a very beautiful, formal party in New York."

"Then he got back in time for the party."

"He wasn't away."

"Oh," I said, hoping my disappointment didn't show. If he hadn't been away, he wasn't my man. "I was under the impression he'd made a trip that day, the day of New Year's Eve."

"You've been misinformed. The trip he took was the day before."

"I see. OK. Was it Atlanta he visited that day?"

"No, he hasn't been to Atlanta for some time. He was up in Boston the day before New Year's Eve. He thought he might have to stay over but he phoned me that night and said he'd got his work done and he'd take the next plane home. He was back when I got up in the morning."

"Do you know who he visited in Boston?"

"No idea. You'll have to ask him. He'll be back after lunch. He's taken the kids out for a while. But whoever it was must have gotten an unexpected bonus from his visit. Jerry lost his favorite pen on the trip and he grouched about it all morning. It must have fallen out of his pocket somewhere."

My skin tingled. There had been some pens and pencils at the crime scene and I had assumed they belonged to D.D., but he could have bent over and the pen went rolling. Even if he were wearing gloves the whole time he was in the farmhouse, the pen would still have his prints from the last time he used it. "I know how he must feel," I said sympathetically. "My husband only carries inexpensive pens because he's always lending them and never getting them back."

"Maybe that's how he lost it," she agreed. "And whoever borrowed it decided it was too good to give back. But what does all this have to do with Susan Stark?"

"I'm not sure how it fits," I hedged. "She made some very strange statements when she got back. Tell me, when your husband called, did he use a phone in a hotel or at the airport?"

"He doesn't do that anymore," she said with a smile. "He got himself one of those adorable little cell phones and he uses that. Then he has a record of all the calls at the end of the month."

And so would the police, I thought, grateful for the adorable little phone and the monthly bill that came with it. If he made a call from anywhere in upstate New York between here and Bladesville, that would be the end of his trip-to-Boston story. Not to mention that he would not be able to find anyone in Boston who could vouch for his presence on the thirtieth of December.

"They are cute," I said. "I wish I could afford one."

"It's a matter of safety nowadays. You really can't

afford to be without one. Is there anything else? Susan must be confused if she thinks Jerry went to Atlanta."

"She is confused. I'm glad I was able to straighten it out. Thank you, Mrs. Childs." I stood and picked up my coat. "I was sorry to hear of your father-in-law's death."

"Thank you. He was really a driving force and it was very sudden, very unexpected. One moment he was alive and the next moment, dead. Jerry's been very upset about it. They were extremely close, and Jerry had just been up to visit him when it happened."

"Had his father retired?"

"Oh no. He was the quintessential entrepreneur. He didn't stop working until his heart stopped beating."

"That's quite a tribute," I said with admiration.

We walked through the house to the front door and I thanked her for her help. I wanted to talk to Jack quickly and have him set the wheels in motion. If Mrs. Childs told her husband the substance of our conversation when he returned, he might realize he was a suspect and destroy whatever evidence he hadn't already gotten rid of.

Jack took notes as I talked a few blocks from the Childs house. "That missing pen is a real stroke of luck," he said. "The upstate cops'll have it if it was in that house. There are bound to be prints on it. Once we establish he was in that house, any alibi he may have breaks down."

"And then there's the cell phone."

"That cell phone is going to be a big piece of evidence, too. It'll tell us exactly where he was at a particular time. We ought to be able to get the record of that call pretty quick. He's probably been billed for December already. You did great. What we need to find is the murder weapon or a matching fingerprint on the pen or anywhere else. There were a number of prints in that house that didn't match the victim or Susan."

"Probably some from Teddy Toledo. He dropped by a lot."

"It would be nice if this Jerry Childs left one, too."

"I wonder if he went there to kill her or just to talk to her."

"Could be either. His father must have confided in him before he died."

That had been my thought. "Mrs. Childs said Jerry had just visited his father before the fatal heart attack."

"Old guy unburdens himself and then dies. Son takes up the cause."

"So what do we do?"

"We go to the local police station and get some phone calls made. We need that telephone bill, we need to see if that pen is in custody and if it has Childs's prints, we need a search warrant for their premises for the kind of weapon that killed D.D. Butler."

"Like a shovel?"

"Right. I hope they can get a judge to sign a warrant today. And then we need to bring Childs down to the police station and get him printed. So let's see what we can accomplish."

25

It was fairly complicated, what with all the police departments that were involved. Bladesville said, sure, pick the guy up. The upstate coroner had determined that something like a garden shovel had been the weapon, so that was what the local police would search for at the Childs house, albeit very reluctantly. Jerry Childs was well known in town, well liked, an all-around good citizen. He was pretty far from the usual suspect in a bludgeoning case.

Getting a warrant to search the Childs premises was a lot harder. It isn't easy to get a judge on a weekend. They like their days off as much as the rest of us, and the first one the police tried to contact wasn't home. The second one wanted something more substantial than what he referred to as vague suspicions. Fortunately, while one detective was on the phone with the judge, another detective was able to get a fax of Childs's December cellular telephone bill. Late in the evening of December thirtieth he had called his home number from the central office that served Bladesville. As far as I was concerned, we had him. The judge apparently agreed and said he would sign a warrant.

When the detective talking to Bladesville was finished, Jack got on the phone and asked whether a pen had been found in the house. There was a lot of discussion and a pause while, I assumed, questions were asked about whether a pen had been logged in. He hung up looking unhappy.

"Pencils and ballpoints," he said. "Nothing that a man would notice was missing."

"Unless he patted his shirt pocket the way I've seen you do and realized that the cheap little pen he'd had in the morning wasn't there and he had a good idea where he'd lost it."

Jack gave it a second's thought. "He wouldn't mention it to his wife. It must have been a decent pen, maybe one she gave him as a gift. Let's see if we can hold his attention before the cops come to execute the search warrant."

We drove back to the Childs house but the empty space in the garage was still empty. Then I saw a child in an upstairs window.

"He's come and gone, Jack."

"Uh-oh." He stopped in front of the house and we dashed up the front steps.

Mrs. Childs opened it. "Can you tell me what's going on?" she said, looking distressed.

"Where's your husband?" I asked.

"I have no idea. He came home a little while ago and when I told him you'd been here he got very upset. Then I said something about his missing pen and he just—" She held her hands apart, indicating she had no more idea where he was than we did.

"He took off," Jack said.

"Yes, but why?"

"Come on, Chris. Thanks, Mrs. Childs." He started moving back toward the car and I ran after him. "Want me to drop you at the police station and ask them to take you home?"

"You'll lose him. Just go. I know the best way to get there."

* * *

It was one of those moments when I wished we had a phone in the car. We should have called ahead to Blades-ville for a welcoming committee to greet Mr. Childs, but we couldn't take the time. Jerry Childs had probably made this trip in the dark and might have to slow down to look for landmarks. I had done it during the day and somewhat more recently than he had and I was sure I would recognize every turn.

When we got there, a black Mercedes was parked up near the house and Jack pulled in tight behind it to keep Childs from fleeing.

"Stay back," he said to me, and I watched the other personality take over, the one that was all business. He took the off-duty revolver he was carrying from the belt holster, went quietly up the steps, moved to the side, and opened the door.

When he was inside I followed him up the steps and into the foyer, listening for a sound that would tell me where Jack was. I didn't want to go any farther in case Childs showed up, although I was pretty sure he wasn't armed. All he wanted to do was find the missing pen and get out. He wasn't expecting a confrontation and surely didn't want one.

And then I heard it, loudly. "Police! Don't move!"— the universal phrase. It had come from the kitchen and was followed by exclamations and sounds of disgust and fear.

"What's your name?" Jack shouted.

"Jerry Childs. William J. Childs. Who the hell are you?"

"Down on the floor," Jack shouted.

"What the hell is going on?"

"Mr. Childs, you're under arrest for the murder of Delilah Butler," Jack said, as I walked with relief and confidence toward the kitchen. He recited the Miranda warning as the man complained loudly.

When I got to the door of the kitchen, I saw that he was sitting uncomfortably on the floor, handcuffed by his left hand to one foot of the old iron stove that had given D.D. her only heat.

"You OK?" Jack said as he saw me.

"Fine."

"Don't touch anything. We're going to do this by the book." He turned to his prisoner. "You got that cute little cell phone you always carry with you?"

Childs reached into his pocket with his free right hand, pulled something out, and tossed it to Jack.

"Thanks. This will spare you a trip," he said to me. Then he opened it up, dialed the police, and we sat back and waited.

It didn't take them long. Two uniformed deputies came into the house and introduced themselves.

"We're looking for a pen," Jack explained. "The suspect here may have lost it when he murdered the Butler woman."

"I thought they had a girl in New York for that," one of the officers said.

"They have no case. Chris, you have any idea where to look for that pen?"

"It could have rolled under the mattress or behind one of these cabinets."

The men started looking, poking around, sticking their hands beneath and behind anything movable or slightly off the ground. There was no pen under the stove, under the mattress, under any of the clothes still piled on the floor. They moved, pushed, reached, and poked. No pen.

"There's a bedroom upstairs," I said, "where it looks like she slept in warmer weather. All of her papers were taken. If they were lying on the floor up there, he might have bent over to pick them up. I'll show you where it is."

I led the way up the stairs to the second floor, then to the bedroom with the old dresser and bedframe. I was about to take my little flashlight out of my bag when the deputies both reached for theirs.

The floor of the room was pretty clean, except for dust. They shone the light under the dresser, under the bed, and around the perimeter.

"Let's try the closet," I suggested.

One of them went into it, shining his light on the floor. "Hey," he said. "I think maybe I've got it." He stopped and put a plastic glove on. Then he knelt. When he stood up he was holding something black and shiny. "This what you're looking for?"

"I think you've done it," I said.

They put the pen in a plastic bag, sealed it, made notes on the paper label, and then took Childs into custody. He was angry and confused, more worried, it seemed to me, about his Mercedes than about his future.

"You didn't have to kill her," I said, as they prepared to take him outside.

"I didn't kill anyone. I just talked to her. I told her to leave us alone."

"Was she blackmailing you?"

"Not me, my father. She killed my father. She dug in and she wouldn't let go. There was nothing he could give her that would make her stop. She wanted to destroy his life, his family, my mother especially. She had no right."

"Why did you come up here that particular night?" I asked.

"She told my father to come on New Year's Eve in the morning. He thought she wanted to kill him, that she'd be waiting for him. I told him I would go instead, come early and surprise her, see what I could do to get her to stop. About an hour after my father and I talked, he had a heart attack and died."

"I'm sorry," I said.

"Not as sorry as I am. I came up here the night before New Year's Eve. I didn't know she lived like this. She was a nobody and she pushed people around. She didn't want to talk. We got into a fight and she hit her head on the stove."

I knew it wasn't true. There was no blood on the stove and she hadn't fallen anywhere near the stove. It was the beginning of a story to keep himself from paying the full price for what he had done.

"I'm not sure she wanted to kill your father," I said, aware that the two local cops were listening with fascination to this unsolicited confession. "She wanted a kind of family reunion."

"She wanted that, too," Childs said. "I found her script for New Year's Eve when I went through the house. The bitch had it all written down like a play, who would say what. It was going to be a massacre. It was crazy."

"Then you knew who the other players were," I said.

"Not for a while. She had them coded. She just called them Mother, Father, Sister. I wasn't included. It was just her half sister she invited. My father never told me the names."

"Did you figure out who the half sister was?" I asked.

"When Susan came back I put it together. I decided it was better to treat her as if she was innocent than make an issue of it. I couldn't see how anyone would ever connect me to this place."

"It took a little doing," I said.

"OK, Mr. Childs, we gotta go," the younger deputy

said. "You got a big mouth on you. One of these days it's gonna get you in trouble."

I couldn't imagine a greater understatement.

26

There was an impromptu party the next day at the Golds'. We took Eddie, and everyone commented on how he had grown in the last seventeen days. It was true. At half a pound a week he was now more than a pound heavier than on New Year's Eve, and he looked much more like a bouncing baby than he had when they had last seen him.

The Starks were there, Ada looking even more worn than she had when I had met her soon after Susan's disappearance. Arnold, who, of course, had learned all the family secrets the easy way from the players themselves, told me when we got there that Ada had finally, after all those years, told her husband for the first time about the child she had given birth to before she met him. Ernie seemed as calm and contented as a man could be. If he had been troubled by her confession, you couldn't see it in his face or demeanor. Somehow Ada had failed to understand that her husband loved her and was unconcerned by something that happened before he came into her life.

"Nobody has to talk about anything," Arnold said as we sat in the living room. "Chris and I want to know everything but that's our problem, right, Chrissie?"

"Right as always, Arnold. We've got it pretty much figured out by now."

"What I don't understand is how you made all those connections," Susan said. She was sitting on the sofa next to Kevin and holding his hand as though she were afraid he would get away if he had the opportunity, but he looked as though he wouldn't leave even if someone pushed him.

"I'm not sure where it really started," I said, "but there were two things that got me going. One was Sister Joseph, the General Superior of St. Stephen's, where I was a nun. She said something about there being so many magazines in this case. Somehow there was a magazine connection that I had to find. The other thing was that when I read that awful story that D.D. Butler wrote, I couldn't believe that a literary magazine—or any other magazine for that matter—would publish it. I mean, it was really terrible. And as it turned out, the editor of the magazine published it because she was asked to. By her father."

"But how did you get to Jerry?"

"By default," I admitted. "I finally got down to his father, who I was sure was the killer. I drove up to Brewster, got into the house to talk to Mrs. Childs, and she told me her husband had died about two weeks before New Year's Eve. For a while I really thought I'd come to a dead end. But when I got home, I called the publisher of the magazine that had printed D.D.'s photo-essay, and he told me Mr. Childs had a son as well as the daughter I had already talked to. I didn't really recognize the first name, but when I heard the name of your magazine, I realized he was my next suspect."

"Well, you did a great job, Chrissie," Arnold said.

"And you must all be hungry," Harriet put in. "Let's sit down and eat. I'm sure we all know how to talk with our mouths full."

I was the one who still had questions. Susan and Kevin

sat across the table from Jack and me. I decided to give it a shot. If she didn't want to answer, I would see it in her face.

"I assume," I said, "that you went to Bladesville the morning of New Year's Eve."

"I did. I had already arranged to borrow Jill's car, and I just got up that morning, had breakfast, and walked over to the garage where Jill kept it. I knew where I was going. I had called the AAA and asked for directions. So I drove up there."

"Did your parents know you'd slept in the house the night before?"

"Sure," she said with total innocence, looking at her parents as though she couldn't imagine why I had asked the question.

"I said I didn't know whether you'd stayed over," Ada said unhappily.

"Well, I did. And I got up to the house where D.D. Butler was staying at maybe ten, ten-thirty that morning. I pulled the car up on the property where it looked like other people had parked—it wasn't plowed or anything—and I rang the bell and knocked on the door. When she didn't answer, I went in."

"I'll bet that's a moment you'll never forget," Jack said.

"Never for the rest of my life. She was lying there, face-down, in that awful cluttered kitchen, blood kind of frozen on the floor. And all I could think was that my mother had done it. I was so scared, I was so confused." She stopped talking and a shudder seemed to run through her.

"You knew who D.D. was," I said.

"I'd known for some time. And I'd known because I saw a couple of the letters she was writing to my mother even before she wrote to me. I figured Mom just reached the end of her rope and killed her."

"And, of course, when I got there, I didn't know for

sure who that was lying on the floor in the kitchen," Ada said. "My first thought was that it was D.D. since she lived there. But who would have killed her? Then I thought, 'What if D.D. invited Susan, too?' D.D. had written me that she was having a 'reunion' on New Year's Eve and I thought she just meant herself and me. But if she had found me, she could just as easily have found Susan. She gets mail at the house all the time and I pass it along. How would I know what was inside? D.D. could have handwritten one envelope and typed the other and mailed them from different places.

"Susan had left before me that morning. Maybe she had come up to that house and gotten in a fight with D.D. and killed her. And then I thought, 'What if that's Susan lying there?' My mind suddenly blanked. I couldn't remember what Susan had been wearing at breakfast, but the body had sneakers on and I was pretty sure Susan had been wearing hers. The hair was all messed up but it was Susan's color. I tried to see the face but there wasn't any face to see. It was terrible."

"Did you think about how Susan had gotten up there?" Jack asked.

"I didn't. I knew Kevin had a car and Susan often drove it. And if D.D. had killed Susan, maybe she drove off in the car Susan came up in."

"Ada, you must have been at your wit's end," Harriet said.

"Beyond that. Way beyond. I was so terrified I didn't know what to do. But I'd told Ernie I was taking the car and doing some shopping so I drove around, stopped for coffee a couple of times, and eventually went home. I didn't know if Susan was dead or alive or what I would say to her if she came home, whether I should try to talk to her about it. I just felt crazy. Then, when Kevin called and asked to talk to her, it hit home. She was going out with him that night, and he was calling to talk to her and she wasn't there. And she didn't come home and didn't come home and I was left with those two terrible possibilities, that she was dead in that farmhouse or that she was alive and a killer." Her voice broke on the last word and she bent her head over the table.

"Seems to me," Arnold said from his position at the head of the table, "that the villain in all this was the victim. From what I've learned, a lot of it from Chrissie here, she decided to do what she could to destroy her natural parents and take Susan along for the ride. She must have been a pretty sick person."

"Or very angry," I said. "She had a nice family. I met them."

"It wasn't enough," Ada said. "Nothing was enough. It's very sad."

"It's an amazing story, though," Jack said. "She took years to infiltrate herself into the lives of these people she was related to by blood, pushed them around, showing how superior she was to them. And then she got them all to go up to that house for her reunion."

"Did Jerry Childs still have that play of hers?" I asked him.

"I talked to the Bladesville cops this morning. Tenafly hasn't been able to find anything like that. But they did find the murder weapon."

"You've been holding out on us, Jack," Arnold said.

"Just looking for the right moment. It was a shovel, and he must have put it in his car because there are traces of blood in the trunk. As the autopsy indicated, it must have been the shovel she used to clean out the wood-stove. There's ash and charcoal on it. He isn't saying anything."

"After the speech he made at the farmhouse, he should

be very careful what he says." I couldn't imagine any lawyer letting him go on as he had yesterday afternoon.

"He says he found a loaded gun in that kitchen," Jack said. "Probably what she intended to use when her 'guests' arrived the next morning. She didn't have it handy or Jerry might not be among the living."

"And D.D. would," Arnold said. "Where's the alleged weapon?"

"He told the police he stopped on the Tappan Zee Bridge on his way home and tossed everything into the Hudson River—at its widest point, of course. I doubt they're going to dredge the river for it."

There was a cry and everyone stopped talking.

"Sounds like a hungry baby." I pushed my chair away from the table and started for the stairs.

"Bring him down when he's finished," Harriet called.

"And tell the folks how you stood up for women's rights singlehanded against a whole police force," Arnold said.

"OK. See you all later." I hurried up the stairs. "Coming, little sweetheart," I said, as I reached the second floor.

27

It was dark when we got home, and time for bath and bed for our youngest member. The answering machine was flashing, but I didn't have time to listen so I asked Jack to. He came into Eddie's bedroom while I was bathing him.

"They're charging Jerry Childs with second-degree murder."

"That sounds fair. I doubt he planned it, although he was pretty angry after his father's death."

"If he'd shot her with a gun he brought along, they'd have a case for first-degree, but with a shovel he found in her kitchen you can't prove he went up there to kill her."

"I wonder if she intended to kill all three of them," I said, lifting Eddie out of the water and wrapping a soft towel around him. "Mm, don't you smell sweet."

"Where's his weapon?"

"Gone with the papers D.D. had. Gone with the alleged gun he found in her kitchen. If Jerry destroyed all that, he could have tossed his own gun, too."

"He didn't toss the shovel."

"True. But it was in the trunk, remember? It's not easy to open your trunk at the side of the Tappan Zee Bridge and pull out a shovel."

"So we'll never know. That is some gorgeous kid, Chris. Look at that face."

I kissed the little face and smoothed powder on his velvety skin. "You are really something," I told him.

"Oh, and there's a message from Mel. Wants you to call."

"After I put Eddie to sleep." I took him on my lap, and started to nurse.

Mel answered on the second ring. "Chris! Hi. How are you?"

"Tired but happy. Eddie's sleeping and we're too full to eat dinner. How are you guys?"

"We're fine. Listen. I miss you terribly. Why don't I see you anymore?"

"I hate to bother you when you're working all day. I miss you, too. It's just—you know, you're working, you have so much to do. . . ."

"Ridiculous. Come over tomorrow, OK? Four o'clock?"

"I'll be there."

"And I want to hear everything, all about the case."

"There's more, Mel. I was almost arrested for indecent exposure when I nursed Eddie in my car upstate."

"You're kidding."

"No, really."

"Tomorrow. Make it three-thirty."

I took a deep breath. "I'll be there."

Even after leaving the cloistered world
of St. Stephen's Convent for suburban
New York State, Christine Bennett still finds
time to celebrate the holy days.

Unfortunately, in the secular world
the holidays seem to end in murder—
and it's up to this ex-nun to discover
who commits these unholy acts.

LEE HARRIS

The Christine Bennett Mysteries

Published by Fawcett Books.
Available in your local bookstore.